PLANETFALL

A STORY OF THE DARK

J A SUTHERLAND

DARKSPACE PRESS

PLANETFALL
A Story of the Dark

by J.A. Sutherland

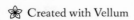 Created with Vellum

Denholm Carew enjoys a life most would envy. Scion of a wealthy family on New London, he can have almost anything he wants. But what he wants more than anything is the freedom to make his own way and build his own legacy to pass down to his children. Together with his wife, Lynelle, he sells everything to buy shares in colonial company and settle the newly discovered world of Dalthus IV.

For the Readers.

This may be a bit hokey and all, but when I released the first book in this series, I had a rather modest idea of what I'd consider its "success". The response from you, the readers, has been far beyond what I could have hoped for.

I'm thrilled that so many of you enjoy this series, and hope to continue with you for many books and years to come.

FOREWORD

Planetfall is a prequel to the Alexis Carew series, which starts with *Into the Dark.* If you're new to the series, I strongly suggest starting with *Into the Dark,* rather than *Planetfall,* as this story was written more for someone who's already a fan of the series and is interested in more background on some of the characters and customs.

Also, *Planetfall* is available free to subscribers to my mailing list ... so there's that.

J.A. Sutherland

PART ONE
NEW LONDON SYSTEM

ONE

Saying goodbye to an entire planet is harder than I thought.

Denholm Carew rested his hands on the balcony rail and looked out over the city he'd called home for his entire twenty-two years of life. A light breeze ruffled his hair and he was tempted to turn off the static wall that blocked most of the winds from reaching him, but a glance at the wind gauge put paid to that idea. Anything up to fifty kilometers would have him at the rail, teeth bared and exhilarated, but the winds today were topping one hundred fifty, gusting out of the nearby mountains and funneling through the canyons made by Shrewesport's tall buildings.

He looked down to the ground over a hundred stories below and smiled sadly. He was going to miss this place. With a population of just over twenty million, it wasn't New London's largest city, but he'd called it home for a very long time. And then fought like hell to leave it forever.

Denholm felt hands on his back that slid along his sides to the front and pulled him into an embrace.

"Second thoughts, love?"

He turned around and wrapped his own arms around his wife, Lynelle. His smile turning from sadness to delight as he stared into her bright green eyes.

"Second. Third. Fourth. And more," he admitted. "You?"

Lynelle ducked her head to lay it against his chest, her long dark hair tickling his chin.

"You overthink things, love," she said.

There had always been a bit of the New Edinburgh system in her speech, the slightest hint of a burr, though her family'd been on New London proper for three generations. She hid it well in New London's Society, not wanting to be looked down upon, but he'd found it came out more and more frequently as their departure date grew nearer.

The New Edinburghans, even hundreds of light years removed from their native Scotland, were a proud bunch and resistant to change. New Edinburgh had been settled during the expansion of nationalist colonies and had remained fiercely independent despite New London's growing influence. It was only after all of the surrounding systems had come under New London's rule that they'd finally given in and agreed to inclusion in the kingdom.

"It's decided to go a'colony when just a wee lass, I did," Lynelle reminded him. "And nae looked back for myself."

Denholm pushed her away and raised her chin so he could look her in the eye again. "From a wee lass? Nigh a hundred years has it been, then?"

Lynelle growled at him and snapped her teeth at his hand. "Planned t'be gone at eighteen, so don't be making me regret the year more I've waited through your hemming and hawing."

Denholm grinned and leaned down to kiss her. Not the chaste peck on the cheek that would be approved of by New London's fashionable set, but a full, deep, passionate kiss. One he hoped would leave her with no doubt of just how much he loved her — and how lucky he felt he was to have found her.

For years, he'd used his dream of leaving New London to found a colony as a foil, something to fend off the parade of marriageable dunces his family had trooped in front of him. Tell one of those hothouse flowers that he planned to sell up every bit of wealth he had to buy shares in a colony and ... well, those that understood what was involved had coughed, excused themselves, and never been seen again. Those that hadn't understood had, at least, been worth a laugh or two.

"What? Farm? In the dirt, do you mean?"

"Would we still be able to make it to The City of an evening?"

"Whatever is a cow?"

That last had been the topper, for when he'd asked her where she thought beef came from, she had, with absolute seriousness, replied, "Well, from Cook, of course, but she knows I prefer chicken."

Lynelle's response had been to pull out her tablet and begin discussing the pros and cons of the colony world brochures she'd already reviewed. Not a word of it that Denholm had remembered the next day, for he'd spent those hours simply staring at her, entranced that he'd found someone who shared his dream. He'd finally gotten over his daze enough to pay attention, and they'd spent two years going over the brochures and survey reports for each newly discovered world.

They'd married, announcing on their wedding invitations that, in lieu of gifts, guests could purchase them shares in the Dalthus Colonization Company. And, not incidentally, that all of Denholm's and Lynelle's trusts, family holdings, and possessions were being liquidated to the same purpose, so if you want that silver service of Great Aunt Mathilda's then you should make an offer before the whole lot's up for auction.

And now it was finally time.

"We should go," Lynelle whispered.

Denholm nodded. They left the balcony and entered the apartment they'd shared since they'd married. It was empty now, all of the

furnishings sold to buy one last fraction of a share or to pay the shipping on one last kilo of freight to make their start. Even the apartment
had been sold, its walls already set to a neutral beige in preparation
for the new owners and whatever their tastes were.

The Carew family's long time solicitor, Beal Silvers, was waiting
by the door.

"All set, Denholm?" he asked.

"Surprised you came, Beal," Denholm said, taking the man's
hand. "But I appreciate it."

Beal looked a bit sad at that. "I wouldn't let you leave without
saying goodbye, Denholm."

"Why not when my own blood will?"

Beal pursed his lips. "Yes, well, the family would rather I had you
declared incompetent. Your sister asked why I couldn't place you in a
nice asylum somewhere and simply *tell* you it was another planet.
They're quite convinced you'd never know the difference."

"They'd bloody well ken the difference when I was done with
them," Lynelle said.

Beal laughed. "There's more than one of them who's that afraid
of you, Lynelle."

"Well I am glad you came, Beal," Denholm said.

"Mind you," Beal said, "I do think you're barking. Stubborn,
wrong-headed, reactionary, and stark, bloody, barking mad."

Denholm grinned. "But?"

Beal grinned back. "Every New Londoner's natural right to be so,
family approval or no," he said. "How else does one explain the
farthing?"

Denholm laughed. The putative insanity of New London's
founders was a common position. They'd settled the world with the
belief that a strong monarchy and a hereditary aristocracy based on
each family's shares in the founding corporation were a fine form of
government. Moreover, they'd abandoned simple, decimal currencies
in favor of an archaic system that drove the merchants mad.

Denholm clapped Beal on the shoulder. "Will you ride with us to the spaceport, then?"

"What I came for," Beal said. "A few last bits of business we should discuss, yes?"

TWO

The three of them left the apartment and made their way down the hallway to the aircar landing. As they stepped out onto the landing, Denholm said, "I was rather looking forward to a public car, you know, Beal? Haven't been in one since I was at school."

"They haven't changed much since then — mine's much more comfortable," Beal said, gesturing for Denholm and Lynelle to precede him to the car.

The landing was open to the air, but protected from the winds by more static fields. Denholm concentrated on the view of the nearby buildings, wondering when he'd ever again see one more than two or three stories tall.

"Wait," he said as they neared the car. His eyes narrowed. "That's my car!"

Beal stepped close enough for the car's door to open and shrugged. "No longer — told me to sell everything for you, after all."

Lynelle laughed. "Did he give you a fine deal on it, Beal?"

"Quite — but still enough to ship a chicken or two to Dalthus for you," Beal said, prompting Denholm to laugh as well.

"The real money's in the shipping, no doubt," he agreed. "Habitable planets're two a penny compared to the getting there."

They entered the car and seated themselves, Denholm starting to take the owner's seat as he had for years, but then moving on with a chuckle. Beal seated himself there and closed the door.

"Port," he said. "Dalthus Colony departure."

The car lifted smoothly from the pad. It slid through the static field into the winds, but its antigrav generator and inertial compensators kept the ride smooth for the occupants. It slipped easily into the traffic patterns and headed for the spaceport.

"The shipping rate the colony company negotiated is about what I'd expect," Beal said. "Still bloody usury, though, when you get down to it."

Denholm shrugged. "It's a far distance for their ships and little cargo for the return, at least until they get back to the Zariah system. They're established enough there to have some exports."

"Even so," Lynelle added, "there'll not be enough there to fill thirty ships." She leaned close to Denholm and he wrapped an arm around her automatically. "Were they mine, I'd nae send them back all together. Have them take different routes so they'd have *some* cargo, at least."

"The shipping company claims its safer," Denholm reminded her, "in case of pirates."

Lynelle made a rude noise. "I've read the reports they sent along. Pirates, my —" She grinned wickedly, "— arse."

Beal looked at her in shock, but Denholm chuckled. He was used to Lynelle's ... earthier language, in private. Language that would make the prim, fashionable set of New London society faint dead away.

"What, then, Beal?" Lynelle asked. "I'm tae be a farm-wife, nae some proper lady, and free to speak as one." She grinned again, the wicked one that made Denholm know she'd be doing as she liked and expecting him to 'apologize' for her after. "A'times there's no *proper* word but —"

"Please!" Beal cried, holding up a hand to forestall her. He cleared his throat. "Leave me my illusions, at least?"

Lynelle pouted and Denholm realized that her burr was more pronounced too, as though she were already throwing off the conventions and requirements of New London society the closer they came to leaving. He knew she'd had to keep both her language and accent in check to avoid being looked down on by their social set, only relaxing her guard in private with him or her own family, but only now began to suspect just how much of an effort that might have been for her. *Always having to pretend, so as not to be looked down upon.*

"Bless ya, lass," Denholm said, putting on an exaggerated accent himself in support of her. "Soon it's ever' improper word y'like, y'cn be sayin'."

Lynelle pulled back and stared at him for a moment. She rested one hand gently on his chest.

"'At was a brogue, love … and a poor one." She shook her head quickly. "Dinnae try agin', please? There's nary a bit o'Celt in you." She settled back against him and looked at Beal. "The pirates're made more of than they are," she said. "Proper armed and crewed, one ship could stand 'em off."

"There is that," Beal agreed, "but men and arms require more coin each voyage."

Lynelle nodded. "And these merchants'll ship no more crew than they need to make sail." She snorted derision. "And arms that'll do more harm tae their own. Lasing tubes all cracked 'n fair t'blow apart. Shot that'll nae hold a charge … or t'won't seal against *darkspace*." She sighed. "Penny-wise 'n pound-foolish, the lot of 'em."

Denholm hugged her tightly. "You've thought on that a bit. Perhaps we should sell off our shares and buy a ship?" he teased. "Be my first mate?"

Lynelle raised an eyebrow. "You, the captain?" She grunted. "No, you can be *my* bosun — keep the hands in line, like." She dug a finger into his ribs. "An' I'll be your only *mate*, if y'ken what's good for you, love."

Beal cleared his throat. "As may be," he said, "but that business I spoke of?"

Denholm and Lynelle nodded to indicate he had their attention.

"Good, then. I've kept the investigators working," Beal said, "right up to this last minute. So far as we can tell, the Dalthus Company is entirely commercial. None of the other shareholders seem to have any agenda or politics to speak of."

Denholm nodded and he felt Lynelle sigh with relief. They'd been fairly sure of that, but one could never be entirely certain. Even if a colony venture had no overt biases, there was always the possibility of a small group hidden within the larger. Colonies had changed a great deal since the very first ones, in some ways becoming even more complicated.

When humanity first found habitable planets, the governments of Earth saw them as a fresh start. A way to show that people, no matter their histories, could start over without the petty hatreds and bigotry that had caused so much misery on Earth. Both Terra Nova and *Nueva Oportunidad* had been founded with those ideals. Colonized with people from all over the world, carefully selected by the best experts available, and thrown together to make a fresh start on brand new worlds.

The wars had been violent, bloody, and filled with atrocities on all sides.

All, not both, for there were dozens of sides involved. All willing to ally with others, for a time, in an effort to get rid of "those bastards" ... whichever bastards those happened to be. The fact that there were so few colonists seemed to make it worse, not better. Despite an entire planet to spread out on, the thinking seemed to be, "Well, there aren't many of *them* are there? So if we kill them all *now*, we'll have a whole planet free of the bastards!"

Then the reports from further survey ships had come in. Habitable planets were not, in fact, so rare as first suspected. They were, to tell the truth, almost embarrassingly prevalent. Oh, not every star system held one, but there were enough that people began to think quite differently about them. No longer as a scarce, rare resource that, of course, should be managed by proper government regulation, but as something quite common. It was a short leap from that to wondering why governments should be involved at all. History, after all, was filled with examples of governments "discovering", and claiming, new lands ... most of which examples had not turned out terribly well.

There were already private ships that were capable of entering *darkspace* — that odd, terrifying realm that allowed travel between star systems — so why couldn't they explore? And once a habitable system was found by a private ship, why couldn't that company claim it as its own? And, once claimed, why couldn't it be sold?

Want to live somewhere free of those bastards, whomever your particular bastards might be? Get together with your other, right-minded fellows and buy a planet. Buy the whole system — star to Kuiper belt. Dislike your government — whatever that may be? Have a better idea of how to do things? Well, gather your right-minded fellows together and make a go of it with a settled, homogeneous population.

The wars had been violent, bloody, and filled with atrocities on all sides.

Humanity, it seemed — especially those with a strong, passionate certainty that they were right-minded — needed someone to hate and blame. If those bastards — be they a race, ethnicity, religion, or political philosophy — were taken out of the equation then, well, it must be somebody else's fault. And as soon as we've identified those new bastards and got them dead, well, *then* it'll be all right, yes?

The colonies that seemed to prosper, or at least not devolve into civil war, were those whose members, really, just wanted to be left alone. "You farm your land, I'll farm mine, and if you need a hand now and again — and not too bloody often, mind you — well, I suppose that's all right."

There were still many of the other sort, though, who had very set ideas about how things should go. Denholm and Lynelle had tossed all those immediately, but worried about the others. Where a group hadn't *quite* the means necessary to buy a system outright, but *could* scrape together a majority, or super-majority, depending on the colony's charter, to push things their way. They didn't want to find, after the last shuttle had lifted from the planet's surface, that they'd landed themselves into a developing theocracy or political commune.

Or one of the truly *crazy ones*, Denholm mused.

New London, despite its success and eventually becoming the capital of a whole kingdom of star systems, had originally been founded by a group who'd thought a powerful monarchy and heredi-tary aristocracy, along with a quite liberal *code duello*, were fine ideas. That it had somehow managed to work for several hundred years didn't belie the fact that it was lunacy.

Not to mention bringing back the bloody farthing, he thought. *It's not a surfeit of sanity they were having.*

"And you've a fair number of shares between you," Beal contin-ued, "so should be able to strongly influence any votes. There's four others have larger interests than you, though, and a dozen who have nearly as much — enough that you're a force to be reckoned with."

"Not going so as to muck about in politics," Denholm said. "If I wanted that headache I'd stand for Parliament here, as the family wanted."

"Mmh, yes," Beal said. "About the family ..." He sighed. "Your Cousin Reginald's head of the family, once you leave, you know — and he's ... well ..."

"Disowned me, has he?"

Beal nodded. "Made it clear, at least, that once you board the shuttle, you've no further tie to them. Not to come running to him for help, as he put it."

"Bastard."

"*Denholm!*" Lynelle said. "He's your kin, no matter what he thinks of you. Dinnae stoop for him."

"Only the truth, love. Aunt Alfreda let him in the house and raised him, for she couldn't bring forth an heir for Uncle Dorion, but cover it though they might, we all know Reggie came out the wrong side of the blankets." He shrugged. "And the better part of him was left running down Uncle Dorion's leg, to tell the honest truth."

"*Denholm!*"

Beal covered his mouth with one hand and looked away. Whether shocked or to cover a laugh, Denholm couldn't tell, but he suspected both.

"I am going to miss you, Denholm," Beal said when he'd recovered. "To business, though, as we're almost to the port. The gist of Reginald's decree is that you've no call on family funds or resources once you leave. That includes my services, by the way, as paid for by the family." He met Denholm's eye. "Which if you've need of, you've but to write and I'll do all I can for you. Reginald may rant, but I'll not charge you a pence."

"Thank you, Beal, I appreciate that."

"Yes, well, in any case, there are some things I'm sure you've thought of, but I'd feel remiss if I didn't mention them."

Denholm could see him gather himself after having come perilously close to expressing more emotion than was strictly proper for a New London gentleman, especially to one who'd been, at least ostensibly, his employer.

"You'll be careful in your indentures, won't you?" Beal asked. "And keep the colony at large from becoming too desperate in accepting them?"

Denholm nodded, but felt Lynelle stir.

"That's the one thing I dislike about the whole idea," she said. "It smacks of slavery and I dinnae like the taste."

"Nor do I," he said, "but it's the way of it."

Most colonies had some sort of indenture system to bring in more people. Once those who had the funds or skills to buy shares in the colony had been landed, the indentures would begin arriving. Shiploads of those too poor or unskilled to afford even a single share.

Without even the means to pay their passage, perhaps having accrued debt on their homeworld, they'd ship out for the colonies in hopes of a fresh start. The holders there would buy their services, paying off the cost of the passage and any debts in return for an indenture — years of service that would pay off those outlays before the new arrival would be free to make their own way.

More than those, though, would be the ones who'd been given no choice in their indenture — or, rather, that the choice was to either board the indenture ship or enter the gaol.

Beal nodded. "You'll need hands to work your fields, your mines, your mills ... more hands than you think, until you've built up an infrastructure to produce proper, modern machines. Can't rely on buying them in, after all, when you're months away from a world with a factory."

"I ken," Lynelle said. "I do, but it's so like buying the man." She shuddered. "And the abuses ..."

"Not on our lands," Denholm assured her.

The car was descending, almost to the port now, and Denholm could see the rows of shuttles parked and ready to load. The last of the thirty ships the settlers had hired had arrived in orbit the day before and, with that, the call had gone out that it was time to depart. The car landed outside the terminal and Beal stepped outside with them. He held out his hand to Denholm, for he'd not follow them into the terminal itself, then to Lynelle, who pushed his hand aside and wrapped her arms around him.

"Thank you for all your help, Beal," she said.

Beal cleared his throat as she released him, flushing. "Of course, Lynelle, of course."

Denholm took Lynelle's hand and they were at the doorway before Beal called out again.

"Denholm!" They turned back and Beal squared his shoulders. "Your father would be proud of you," he called. "Your mother'd be throwing a proper fit, but Chadburne would be damn proud."

THREE

Denholm and Lynelle entered the terminal. There were a confusing multitude of corridors, some with sliding walkways, branching off the main terminal area, but the building recognized their tablets as they entered and a voice sounded near them.

"Welcome, Mister and Mistress Carew. Please follow the purple line to Dalthus Company embarkation."

A line of purple light appeared on the spotless white floor near them, leading off to one of the corridors. As they stepped forward, the line extended, disappearing behind them.

"Now remember," Denholm teased, remarking on their last bit of training for colonization, a week of orienteering in a New London national park. "There'll be no such directions and paths in the forests of Dalthus."

Lynelle jabbed him in the ribs, flushing. She'd been quite put out to discover that her sense of direction was, to put it politely, abysmal. She'd kept turning the compass in her hand, twisting it to and fro, while muttering, "No, *that's* North, y'silly thing!"

"I've time on Zariah tae work on it more," she said. "And we'll not be so far into the wilderness at the start."

"No," Denholm agreed. "Not until we've better transport imported. And there'll be the satellite constellation we're bringing along, so long as it operates."

The purple light led them to another open terminal and then down yet another corridor, this one not as nicely appointed as the first. In fact, it was quite bare and utilitarian, more suited to cargo than passengers. Which is where they were led in the end, through wide double doors that opened into a vast warehouse full of people and pallets of goods.

"Your personal goods are located in bays C-47 to C-62, Mister Carew" the same voice that had welcomed them said. "Please confirm their contents prior to loading. Once confirmed, you may follow the purple line to livestock confirmation and then to boarding."

"Thank you," Denholm said automatically, though he knew the voice was only the terminal's computer.

He followed the purple light down the pathways between pallets of goods, nodding hello to the other settlers. Most he'd met only briefly, but even those he knew well were more concerned about confirming their belongings were packed than chatting. This was their last opportunity to ensure everything was correct before departing — once aboard ship, they'd have no recourse for something forgotten other than to purchase it on Zariah, assuming it was available, or to order it shipped in with the second wave of supplies and indentures, which would mean a six month wait or more to receive it.

They found their pallets and began checking the contents, Denholm ticking items off on his tablet while Lynelle crawled over and behind the pallets to confirm what was packed on each.

The pallets contained all of their personal goods. Steel plows and fittings for harnesses, a pair of lightweight, plastic wagons, disassembled and packed small, along with the fittings to build two more from wood on the planet's surface. Piping and electrical wire that it would be years before the colony was able to produce in quantity on its own. Solar and wind generators for their homestead, though the colony's shared goods included a fusion plant. It would be years, again, before that plant's power could be transmitted to any great distance from the landing site. An electrical forge and all the metal-working tools necessary for a small homestead — all the tools of any sort, in fact. For mining, lumber, farming, and a host of other activities — all needing to be shipped in until the colony had at least the beginnings of industry for its own.

A few, very few, personal items that they couldn't bear to part with. *Very* few, as the cost of shipping them so far was dear and they knew every last bit of mass they could afford should be spent on something that might make the difference between life and death in the first few years.

Once they confirmed everything was packed and ready to be loaded, the purple light appeared on the floor again and they followed it out of the warehouse and down another corridor. Their destination became clear before they'd even arrived at the next warehouse, for the corridor filled with the scents and sounds of animals. They entered the next warehouse to find the makings of a veritable fleet of arks. Irate ones, to be sure, as none of the animals appeared entirely pleased at their new circumstances.

Feathers and fur filled the air, along with the sounds of chickens, geese, lowing cows and oxen, barking dogs, and a host of others. They seemed to know these new circumstances heralded something even more unpleasant and didn't hesitate to voice their distress. The stench, though, was the worst.

Lynelle covered her mouth and gagged. "Lord, love!" she said. "'T'weren't as bad as this at the farms when we selected 'em."

Denholm tried to breathe shallowly through his mouth, so as to avoid the worst of the smells. "Too many and too close together. And it'll be worse aboard ship." He coughed. "At least they won't be aboard the passenger ships."

"Your assigned livestock bays are LC-17 through LC-36, Mister Carew." Even the terminal's computer seemed to express distaste for the conditions and wish to have as little to do with the place as possible.

This time Lynelle led the way to follow the purple light, striding purposefully and quickly. Denholm followed, marveling at the sheer number of beasts that crowded the warehouse.

Least the beehives're enclosed!

And the sheer expense.

The animals themselves cost little, but the shipping ... a full grown draft horse, and the feed to keep her sound on the twelve week trip ... *and* the water, no matter the ship's recyclers. Then, almost half as much as the purchase and shipping costs was the insurance — the shipping company had three full ships and animals of their own following the colonization fleet, to replace insured beasts that died in transit or to sell, at a profit, to the colonists who'd shipped none, or too few, of their own. Even the poorest craftsman, who'd "bought" his share with the promise of his skills, would find the need to have a chicken or two in his yard.

And some'll not have realized all they'd need, beasts or equipment, neither.

He was suddenly quite certain that the shipping and colonization companies reviewed each colonist's manifests quite thoroughly, and planned for what they could sell when the man realized his want. No matter the number of lists of essential items made available, there'd be some who'd scrimp now and pay dearly later.

The counting here was easier, at least, with the beasts all visible and no scrambling over a packed pallet of goods necessary. Denholm walked the aisle, checking the count and, as best he could, that they were the animals he'd selected from the farms. Four of the draft horses and a pair for riding, a round two dozen of chickens and geese, both, dairy cows and a pair of cows to pull the plows, and a lone cat for whatever native rodents Dalthus held or for the rats and mice that would surely make their way there, as they had to each of humanity's new worlds.

All of them female, as it was far less expensive to ship the essential means of breeding than a full stallion or bull.

He'd considered sheep, if only just for the excuse of having a dog or two along, but there were other colonists better suited to that — he'd learned his first day reviewing a sheep farm that those beasts were bloody stupid and not nearly worth the effort they'd take of him.

Pigs, though, he thought, moving on to the last pen, *pigs're ...*

"Och, love!" Lynelle cried, holding both hands to her mouth. "Whatever were you thinking?"

Well, pigs're smart ... but filthy as sin when penned.

"Was thinking of ham, love," Denholm said. "And bacon of a morning."

He eyed the pen and its filth-covered inhabitants a moment. He was standing near the trough, and the pigs, knowing full well what a human by the trough usually meant, were crowding and jostling each other to get a place. They climbed over each other, smearing the contents of their pen everywhere.

"Bacon's worth a bit of ... well isn't it?"

PART TWO
ZARIAH SYSTEM

FOUR

"Lot 13665!" the loudspeaker announced. "With his pick, Holder Mylin selects lot 13665 — four thousand hectares of prime hillside and *varrenwood* tracts! The next pick belongs to Holder Carew — you have five minutes' time, Holder Carew!"

Denholm grimaced and looked around the crowded field for Mylin. He'd wanted that lot — it stood between two other tracts of *varrenwood* he'd already selected, and getting the third would have allowed him lock up the prime sources of the soon-to-be valuable wood closest to the planned spaceport.

The wide, empty plane outside of Zariah's port city — town, really, as the three thousand colonists for Dalthus almost doubled the town's population — was covered with tents, corrals, and temporary buildings. They'd have a full month here before continuing on to Dalthus, using the somewhat established colony of Zariah to recover from the first part of their passage, fatten their animals and let them regain some of the muscle they'd lost after so long aboard ship, and, as they were doing now, divide the Dalthus system between them. Most of the colonists, at least one from each family, filled the open space around a large vidscreen and loudspeakers for the selections. The vidscreen showed the selections and the order of the next picks, as the colonists milled about waiting their turn.

They'd waited until Zariah to do this so as to meet the survey ships they'd sent to take a more thorough look at the system and have the most recent data to use in choosing their lots. Over four million lots. From tiny, thousand meter square lots in the planned port city to percentages of fishing rights that spanned all of Dalthus' oceans to great swathes of the system's asteroid belt that were measured in light-minutes. Selection of most lots had been simple. The colonists had indicated which of the four million they'd wished and if there were no conflicts then the assignments were made. Where two or more colonists wished a given lot, though, those had been placed into a lottery where they were picked one at a time.

Most important, though, at least in the first generation or two after landing, were the lots that might hold something valuable enough to export — the colony would grow food, of course, for export back to the hungry Core Worlds, perhaps even as far as New London itself, but those were bulk goods and would buy them little more than subsistence.

Varrenwood, though, the huge tree native to Dalthus, had a grain and hue that had already been talked about on New London when they'd gone aboard ship. It was the sort of thing — new, rare, and, most importantly, expensive — that the wealthy Coreward would pay well for. The rarity and expense would set the buyers apart as being at the height of fashion and society — something Denholm dearly wished to take advantage of.

"Sorry about that, Carew!" A hand fell on his shoulder and Denholm turned to find Sewall Mylin at his side. Mylin was a man in his forties, with three sons to help him work the lands he'd claim on Dalthus. Despite being closer to the man's sons in age, Denholm had come to regard Mylin as a friend. "I suspect you wanted that piece, but I felt the need to diversify my holdings nearest the port."

Denholm waved that away. "No matter," he said. "Bound to happen, even with so many to choose from."

Mylin held out his hand. "So no hard feelings, seeing as how we're to be neighbors?"

Denholm took the offered hand. "Of course not." He considered a moment. "In fact, as we'll need a road out of those hills and a mill to work the wood, shall we share the cost of those?"

Mylin pursed his lips for a moment, then pulled out his tablet and showed a map of Dalthus. "How's this ... share the cost of the road, but you build the mill and I've a half share in it, while I'll take this tract of marsh above the port with one of my picks. It's worthless, near as I can see, but a causeway through it — at my expense — would let us connect both our homesteads *and* the hills to the port. Cut our travel time to near a third of what going around would be."

Denholm nodded. A causeway through that muck would take more effort than a mill, and it would be decades before he had the hands to keep a single mill fully utilized on his own.

"Done," he said, shaking Mylin's hand again.

"And what's your next pick, then?"

Denholm pulled out his own tablet and consulted his list. There were several that would do, but none he dearly wanted. That final tract of *varrenwood* had been the last of what he'd planned for development in his own lifetime. The rest of his choices would be left fallow until his children or grandchildren took over the holding.

Or perhaps a bit of a lark? He looked over the options and smiled. Tracts on the nearest coast were going quickly, with several holders clearly planning to make a go of fishing and planetside shipping. It wasn't something he'd planned for himself, but ... *A house by the sea, to spend a fortnight or two each year? Lynelle does love sailing, and a bit of time on a beach with some fresh caught fish grilling over a fire ...*

He smiled and touched the lot to select it.

"Lot 37481!" the loudspeakers declared almost immediately. "With his pick, Holder Carew selects lot 37481 — four thousand hectares of coastline, sea, and commensurate fishing rights! Next pick belongs to Holder Coalson — you have five minutes time, Holder Coalson!"

"God damn your eyes to hell, Carew!"

Mylin's eyes widened at the shout from the crowd, but Denholm merely sighed.

Again? Truly?

There was a rustling of bodies as the crowd around them shuffled to make way for a man striding toward them. A clearly angry man, pinch-faced, hawk-nosed, and not made more attractive by the narrowed eyes and flush of anger that covered his face. He strode toward Mylin and Denholm, oblivious to the dark looks his jostling and demeanor garnered from the other colonists.

"To bloody hell, I say!"

Mylin leaned close, clasping a hand on Denholm's shoulder, and said, "Do you have need of a second, I'll stand for you."

Denholm raised an eyebrow. "I doubt it will come to a duel, but thank you."

"If ever a man needed a good sticking more than Rashae Coalson, I've not met him," Mylin whispered, as the man was closing on them. "I suspect you'd save yourself, and no small host of others, a deal of heartache if you'd kill him now."

"Well?" Coalson stopped a bare two meters from them and stood, hands on hips, glaring.

"'Well', what, Rashae?" Denholm asked. He kept his voice calm, knowing from two times before this had happened that nothing would calm the man before he'd had his rant. Knowing, too, that use of his given name would enrage Coalson further, but unable to resist a bit of tweaking. Mylin was right about one thing ... what Coalson had already said would be cause for a meeting on New London. One simply didn't speak to another gentleman in that manner, and only a desire to not be the first colonist to shed another's blood kept him from calling Coalson out.

Coalson flushed even darker, his hand darting to his hip where the hilt would be were he wearing a sword. Denholm narrowed his eyes.

Perhaps a bit less tweaking ... but, damn me, if Mylin doesn't have the way of it. Never met a man in more dire need of a puncturing than this one.

"I'll have my due respect from you, Carew. Your familiarity is as unwelcome as your plotting!"

"You'll get what you give, Rashae," Denholm said, "and not a bit more from me. But I'll thank you to take your delusions for a stroll ... well away from me, if you please!"

"Three times, Carew! Three times now you've taken the choice at the top of my list! How do you explain it? What are you about, sir?" For a moment, Denholm thought the man would actually stomp his feet like a petulant child. "I demand ... an answer, sir! This very minute!"

Was he about to call me out, but put it off? Denholm thought, eyes narrow and considering. *Afraid or prudent, one — I wonder which.*

"Answer's 'chance', sir," Denholm said. "As it was yesterday and'll still be tomorrow. Now you've but three minutes to make your own selection, and I'll thank you to leave me be while you do!"

Coalson ground his jaw and seemed to be about to say more, but spun on his heel and stalked off into the crowd.

"You've not seen the end of trouble from him," Mylin said. "Nor the worst of it."

FIVE

Denholm made his way back through the lines of tents and domes that housed the Dalthus colonists. He and Lynelle had a plot against the wall that enclosed the port's field. In the distance, from Zariah's main town, came the odd ululating cry that seemed to characterize Zariah's port city several times a day. That and the onion-topped towers the call came from.

He'd like to get away from the colonists' camp and explore a bit of the town, but it had been made very clear to the Dalthus colonists that such a thing wasn't allowed.

It was only a few years ago, in fact, that Zariah wouldn't have allowed the colonists to land at all and they'd have had to stage from a different world entirely. Zariah was still one of the more insular religious colonies, but the system's position made it a prime spot for both the staging of colonial ventures farther into the Fringe and a trading hub for goods moving to and from the Core Worlds.

Zariah's rulers had seen the profit to be had in such a happy accident, so they'd walled off a portion of the plain around this city and turned it into the system's only open port. Foreign traders and

colonists were limited to the space within those walls and not allowed
out.

Their money, on the other hand ...

The prices charged by Zariahn merchants for everything from a
barrel of flour to a chicken made Denholm wince, and he wondered
that those merchants didn't run afoul of Zariah's strict usury laws.

Must not apply to the fleecing of off-worlders.

He reached the bit of space allotted to him and Lynelle and did a
quick check to see that the animals had food and water. They were
recovering well from their time aboard ship and he'd lost not a one of
them. He thought they'd be in fine shape still after the shorter trip
from Zariah to Dalthus.

Once all of the animals were cared for and set for the night, he
entered their shelter.

"Did the choosing go well, love?" Lynelle asked.

Denholm eased himself into one of the canvas chairs set about
their little, one-room hut. They'd had one pallet of goods prepared
specially for the stop on Zariah, with a lightweight shelter, one they'd
use again on Dalthus, as well, until they'd built a proper house, and
simple furnishings. So many of the colonists had settled for canvas
tents for the start, but Denholm felt the need for solider walls. Survey
ships could never account for all of the native fauna, they simply
didn't spend enough time in a system, and he'd heard tales of the
nasty surprises some colonies had encountered. He wanted walls that
sealed around him and offered a bit of protection.

"I missed that third tract of wood — the Mylins got it." He
accepted a mug of coffee from her and smiled as she busied herself at
the portable stove they'd brought down from the ships. "But we made
a bargain for roads and a mill that'll do right by all of us."

"That's nice. And then?"

Denholm laughed. She'd clearly heard about his run-in with
Coalson from someone. "Well, and if you've heard about it already,
why do I need to tell it?"

"So I'll ken the truth o'the rumors runnin' 'round."

"Rumors?"

"Aye. That Rashae Coalson's a fool and fair hears voices — and a bitter coward, afraid to call y'out, to boot. Or that he called y'out and ye refused. Or y've a grudge agin him, and seek his ruin. Or yer a scoundrel and a rogue, an' plan t'take everyone's favorites. Depends on who's the speaker."

Denholm grunted. So many different rumors might mean that the colonists were forming factions, with him and Coalson as the catalysts. That didn't bode well for the colony's start. "And what do you think?" he asked.

Lynelle grinned and came to sit on his lap, straddling his legs and facing him. Denholm wrapped his arms around her and pulled her close. Yet another reason he'd had a more solid shelter brought down — weeks aboard ship with little space and less privacy.

"Well, and ye are a scoundrel," she whispered, leaning close to kiss him on the neck. "And a rogue." She kissed the other side. "An' a right beast." Denholm groaned as her lips brushed his ear and her hands ran over his chest. "An' got me something pretty, did you?"

Denholm had to laugh. It seemed all of his lot choices had been told back to her before he'd even left the field. He supposed he'd have to get used to neighbors gossiping so, in such a small group. Innocent enough, except for those rumors about him and Coalson.

"A bit of coast, I did," he said.

"With a bluff high enow for a house t'catch the winds?"

Denholm nodded, not trusting himself to speak as Lynelle nuzzled his neck again.

"An' a bit o'beach?"

Denholm's vision blurred, but he managed another nod.

"*Secluded* beach, is it?" Lynelle fairly purred. "Enow t'take the sun in me altogethers?"

Denholm's mind went blank, save for the image of Lynelle and her altogethers on sun-drenched sands.

Lynelle straightened, palms against his chest and clearly pleased at the effect she'd had on him. He slid his hands to her waist and swallowed, though his mouth was quite dry.

"And a bargain with Deakin Honeywell," he managed to say, though his voice was hoarse.

Lynelle's brow furrowed. "Bargain?"

Denholm smiled, apparently not everything he'd managed today had been repeated to her already. Honeywell was a craftsman, come along with only a single share in the colony — enough for a bit of land in what was planned to become a seaport to practice his trade.

"The shipwright," Denholm said.

"Denholm, love?"

"Thinks *varrenwood'll* make a proper ship, while we're reliant on wind for shipping, that is. Enough trees for him to experiment with and the first success is to be ours."

"A ship? But, love, we've been plannin' for exports, not local trade —"

"Boat, really, he says ... enough that two may handle it."

Lynelle's eyes widened and Denholm saw them glisten.

"Yer mad," she whispered. "The expense, the time ... so early on."

"We'll have a foreman and hands within the year," he assured her. "And it'll be that long, at least, before Honeywell has the way of working the *varrenwood*, he says. Time enough for us to settle our lands and take a week or a fortnight. That lot is in the southern hemisphere, so we can go when the home farms are idle for winter and spend some time aboard it."

"'Her', love," Lynelle said, leaning toward him. "Boats're always a 'she' — fickle and temperamental as the sea herself." She kissed him deeply. "Lo! But they'll steal yer soul, all the same."

They kissed again, Denholm relishing the taste of her lips, the feel of her body against him, the scent of ...

"*Och!* Me biscuits!" Lynelle leapt from his lap and rushed to the stove where smoke was starting to seep from the oven. A string of

Gaelic curses flowed from her, making Denholm grin. The fiery spirit that had first attracted him, so much brighter than her peers on New London, seemed to be but the merest banked embers compared to her now. And every new flare made him love her more.

SIX

"Are you certain?" Denholm asked. The field was even more crowded than usual on this, what would probably be the last day of choosing lots. With fewer choices and the fatigue of several days of decision making, tempers were high and most just wanted the exercise done with and behind them.

Lynelle shrugged. "We've more than enow planetside," she said. "The belt's fer the future, an' they'll thank us fer preparin' proper."

Denholm nodded agreement and keyed the selection on his tablet. The lot, a slice of the asteroid belt one degree wide as measured by the system's ecliptic plane and zero degrees matching the course to galactic north. It would run from the planetary-solar Lagrange point 2 on the far side of Dalthus VI, second out from the habitable Dalthus IV, through the asteroid belt to the nearer L3 of Dalthus VII. It was, indeed, an investment for the far future, as it would be decades, if not generations, before mining the belt became worthwhile.

Perhaps if there were gallenium to be had. That metal, essential to protecting ships from the ravages of *darkspace,* would make the mining profitable from the start, even after the expense of having to ship in all of the equipment, but there'd been no trace of it found by the survey ships.

"Lot 1724852!" the announcement came. "With his pick, Holder Carew selects lot 1724852 — one degree of arc at 279 degrees, from the Dalthus VI Lagrange 2 to Dalthus VII Lagrange 3. Next pick belongs to Holder Coalson — you have five minutes' time, Holder Coalson!"

An inarticulate howl of rage sounded across the field, silencing the vast crowd as they looked around in astonishment.

"Oh, hell," Denholm muttered in disgust.

"What is it, love?"

The brief silence was broken by another yell of outrage, this one closer, and the crowd began edging away from Denholm. Some of the bystanders looked uncomfortable while others were grinning openly, ready for another show.

"Rashae *bloody* Coalson," he muttered to Lynelle, nodding in the direction of the shouts. "The man must be mad."

"*How?*" Coalson was close now, almost running through the crowd. "*How,* damn you!"

Denholm remained silent. He wrapped an arm around Lynelle and tried to keep his face impassive, but could feel his lips curl in disgust.

I've had far and more enough of this.

"Who've you paid?" Coalson demanded. "How'd you know? *How?*"

"There's little choice left and fewer of us choosing," Denholm said, hoping beyond hope that anything would calm the man. "It's bound to happen at this point. Damn it, man, I can't be the only one who's taken lots you've had your eye on!"

"In the *belt?*" Coalson's eyes were almost bugging out of his head. Spittle flew from his mouth as he shouted. "There're still lots left on the planet! Plenty! The belt's useless in your lifetime!" Coalson ground his jaws and Denholm stared at him, perplexed. The man himself had chosen more than one lot in the belt already. A few others had, as well. Why was he so incensed at it?

"Unless you know," Coalson said, voice quieter. "How'd you know, Carew?"

"Know what?" Denholm asked. "What the devil are you on about?"

"*Liar!*" Coalson yelled and there were gasps from the crowd of watchers.

Denholm's blood chilled. He was almost bound to call the man out for that. Honor would be satisfied by nothing less, but he was loathe to do so. The factions he'd felt were forming earlier seemed to have solidified more, and that'd not do the colony well. For blood to be spilled on top of it, well, that was the sort of thing that started generations long feuds and tore colonies apart.

"There're few of us, Mister Coalson," he said instead, trying hard to project a calm he didn't truly feel. "And hard, trying times ahead. I'll not be the first to spill another's blood when it'll be all we can do to survive our first years together." He showed Coalson open hands. "Good lord, man, are the trials of opening a new world not enough, that we should seek such strife amongst ourselves?"

"*Coward! Liar!*" Coalson stepped forward.

Crack!

The explosive sound of Lynelle's palm striking Coalson's face cut him off and silenced the murmuring crowd like a gunshot.

"No one'll ever speak o' me and mine so!" Lynelle yelled into Coalson's face. Denholm made to draw her back, away from where she'd stepped to meet Coalson, but she shrugged him off. "Y'want blood? A feud? T'call the clans an' sound the pipes? I'll gie it ye hilt an' all!" She had her hand resting on the hilt of the belt knife she wore and Denholm made ready to grab her if she drew it.

"How dare you!" Coalson yelled, hand to his cheek.

"Lynelle," Denholm said, trying to call her back.

"There's some cannae see sweet reason, love," she said. "Some as use yer want fer it agin ye." She stepped closer to Coalson who stumbled back. "The sort'll see y'don' want blood, an' they'll take it as leave t'do their will." Another step closer, so that she had to look up to see Coalson's face. "Me clan's menfolk save their efforts fer a worthy foe, y'see, Mister Coalson. Babe in swaddlin'd do fer you, I think, but, as I've none t'hand ... well, if it's a meetin' y'want, y'send ta *me*, hear?" She stepped back to stand beside Denholm. "But speak o' me or mine so again, Mister Coalson, sir, an' I'll send t'ye meself."

She smiled, and Denholm felt a chill at the sight. Fire ... well, fire was one thing, but this ...

"I'll be right happy t'gut ya, if yer so sore tired a'living."

PART THREE
DALTHUS IV

Planetfall plus three weeks

SEVEN

"Watch yer step, love."

Denholm barely managed to stop his descending foot and move it to the side to avoid a large pile of horse droppings he'd almost stepped in. The other options for where to step weren't much better, truth be told, what with the ever-present mud.

The survey of their landing site on Dalthus must have been done in a different season, one with considerably less ground water. Within two days of the first boat being unloaded, the "streets" they'd laid out for the encampment had become nothing but mud mixed with a variety of droppings.

They'd have to do something about drainage or find another part of the broad river plain they'd landed on to build the first town.

"Makes one wonder what else the surveys may have got wrong," Denholm said, edging to the side.

"Surveys're never all complete," Lynelle reminded him. "Knew it afore we sailed, we did."

Denholm motioned for her to move more to the edges where fewer animals had been driven through.

"It does make me wonder what else was missed, though."

They passed the large, roped off space near the landing field where the Doakes family had set up the beginnings of their chandlery. Most of the tables were bare already, with settlers filling out their needs from the limited stock. Denholm paused, considering stopping in.

"Along w'ye," Lynelle said, tugging on his arm. "We've enough."

"Do you think so? Perhaps another box of nails ..."

"We've far more nails than y'could hammer in the time a'fore the next ships arrive. He'll have more stock at lower cost then, and our own supplies will be on them as well."

Denholm allowed himself to be pulled away. Lynelle was right, he knew, but he couldn't help but wonder if they'd need more of anything. Both wagons were full to bursting, but he'd hate to find himself lacking something essential in the coming weeks. Once they were at their homestead it would be a full day's ride back to Landing, and that assumed Doakes had any stock left at all to sell by then. From the looks of the crowds around his tables, he might not.

"I suppose you're right," he said finally.

They moved on and the thick mud dragging at his boots made Denholm's thoughts return to the survey reports.

"I could wish the surveyors had taken more time with the wildlife, as well," he said.

In general, habitable planets had been found to have lifeforms which were either generally benign to humanity, in that they could be touched and even ingested without harm, though rarely with any real nutritional value, or those that humans reacted to violently, even to a simple touch. Dalthus was the former, which made it ideal for colonization, but that didn't mean there couldn't be some very nasty surprises lurking in the ecosystem.

Viruses were the worst of the lot, as they had a disagreeable tendency to mutate quickly enough to take advantage of newly arrived hosts. The colony's doctor and his medical equipment were amongst the very first loads brought down from the ships. That equipment had proven quite effective on other colonies in identifying those viruses and producing vaccines.

Of more worry to Denholm, about to set out for a remote homestead, was the possibility of large predators who'd never seen a human nor experienced any reason to fear them.

"Do you suppose a gun or two more might prove useful?" he asked, craning his neck to look back at the chandler's tables to see what might be available.

"Laser and powder rifles, both, an' the means to reload cartridges. I think we've enow, love." She nodded toward Denholm's hip. "An' that flechette y've preened over since we landed."

Denholm rested his hand on the butt of the flechette pistol at his hip.

"It was enough to do for that creature rooting about our baggage last night."

"'T'were a rat, love."

Denholm scowled. "Could be native."

"Not much left to tell, after y'were through with it," Lynelle said, "but 't'were a rat."

"Hmph."

Denholm knew Lynelle was likely correct. What was left of the creature after a burst of flechettes had torn into it wasn't really identifiable, but rats had traveled with humanity to every world they'd settled, no matter the precautions. Short of venting an entire ship to vacuum, there was no way to be rid of them completely and few merchant captains were willing to do so on a regular basis.

Something jarred Denholm's arm, knocking him into Lynelle and they almost fell. There was a shout of outrage from behind them and they turned to find a man sprawled on his back in the mud, glaring at him. Denholm didn't recognize him. That was no surprise, really, as the colonists would know best only those who'd traveled with them on a particular ship. There were three thousand and more families settling Dalthus and, though that number seemed small compared to the billions on their home worlds, there were still many who'd never met.

"What do you mean by that, sir!" the man yelled.

Denholm shared a perplexed look with Lynelle. She shrugged to say she had no idea what the man meant either. Other colonists making their way through the street stopped and watched with interest.

"What do *you* mean?" Denholm asked.

The man struggled to get up, dripping mud and worse, but slipped and landed prone again.

"To call me a cur and knock me from your path, sir!" the man shouted.

He was dressed in rough, common clothes, as all the colonists were, but his manner was one of an affronted gentleman. Most of the colonists were of the wealthier classes, of course, shares in a colony company didn't come cheaply, but not all put on such airs.

"You must have misheard," Denholm said. "I called you nothing ... certainly didn't knock you down." He held out his hand to help the man up. "Come, sir, a misunderstanding, surely. Allow me to —"

The man slapped Denholm's hand aside.

"No misunderstanding!"

"He did!" another voice called out. "I saw it. Shoved the gentleman roughly and called him 'cur'! I saw it myself."

The second man came out of the crowd and helped the first man stand.

Denholm didn't recognize the second man either, but he frowned, suddenly suspicious. He knew he'd said nothing of the sort and that he hadn't struck anyone. If anything, the fallen man had struck Denholm from behind before sprawling in the mud. He felt Lynelle squeeze his arm and he gave her a short nod, but didn't take his attention from the two men.

"I'll have an apology, sir!" the first man demanded.

Denholm sighed.

"Love —"

He shook his head to silence Lynelle. He saw what she'd warn him of as well as she did, but he wasn't the 'aggrieved' party. Unless he was willing to apologize for something he hadn't done, and he was not, there was really only one way this encounter could play out.

"You'll not," Denholm said. "I neither struck you nor said a word, sir, you are mistaken."

"You were witnessed!"

"And I suspect whose pocket your witness came from," Denholm said. "May I have your name, at least?"

"You refuse to apologize?"

Denholm squared his shoulders and took a deep breath.

"I've done nothing to apologize for."

"Then I must demand satisfaction, sir!"

"'Course y'do," Lynelle said. "It's yer master's voice says to, is it nae?"

"Lynelle," Denholm warned. It was bad enough one of them was about to be called out, it needn't be both. He turned back to the man. "You've given me no name, still."

"Courtland Thawley," the man said. "Who should my second speak to?"

Denholm didn't have to consider long, there were few enough men amongst the colonists he'd consider friends.

"Sewall Mylin," he said. "He's a lot in the second quadrant next to my own."

Thawley looked Denholm up and down, then turned and stalked off, the "witness" close behind.

Denholm watched them go silently. Once they were gone, the crowd began to disperse. Lynelle kept her grip on Denholm's arm but said nothing.

Denholm remained silent too.

After a moment, they resumed walking, but remained silent and headed toward their campsite.

As they neared their lot, Mylin came from the back of his, wiping his hands on a rag. He waited for them at the post that marked the boundary between their two lots.

"Denholm," he said, nodding as they drew near. "Lynelle." He scratched his chin. "There a reason Rashae Coalson stopped by to ask about weapons and a meeting with some prat name of Thawley?"

EIGHT

"Gentlemen, may we not arrive at an understanding this morning?"

There was still mist covering Landing's field. Off to Denholm's left the hulking shapes of the ships' boats were just barely visible. Their group had left the town and gone farther into the field, almost to the river itself, in order to achieve some privacy and isolation. Oddly, the footing was better here, near the water, than where they'd set up their camp — likely due to there being less foot and vehicle traffic to wear away the ground cover.

The distance hadn't worked for privacy as they'd hoped, as several dozen colonists and crew from the ships had followed behind them to watch the show. He suspected Lynelle was in that group, though he'd asked her not to come.

Denholm eyed Thawley across the ten paces or so that separated them, but said nothing. It was Mylin's place to speak for him as his second, just as it was Coalson's place to speak for Thawley. Those two stood midway between them with Wickam Doakes, the Landing chandler. It was not so much that the parties trusted him, but, rather, that they distrusted him equally. As well, his ninety-nine year lease on the colony's chandlery franchise made his family the registered Crown agent. He'd see that the proprieties were followed, at least.

"My principal will accept an apology and confirmation that he has been ill-used by the gentleman," Coalson said. "Nothing less."

Mylin looked to Denholm, who shook his head slightly. He'd had enough of Coalson and his coterie. All the jabs and slights on Zariah, more on the ships on their way to Dalthus, and finally Thawley's thinly veiled excuse for a challenge.

Denholm had had enough.

"My principal will offer neither," Mylin said.

Doakes shook his head sadly.

"Gentlemen, we've been on-planet barely a week. Is this how our world shall start?"

"Get on with it, Doakes," Coalson said. "I've put off my breakfast for this."

Denholm looked at Thawley, who seemed less sure of himself than Coalson. Thawley opened his mouth to speak, but Coalson went on.

"Struck down into the mud and scoffed at," Coalson said, looking at Thawley. "Would any man's honor stand that without an apology? What would a man's peers think of him after?"

Thawley's jaw clenched and he straightened his shoulders.

"An apology and admission," Thawley said to Coalson. "Nothing else will satisfy."

Denholm shrugged. There was nothing for it, then, for he'd provide neither. He could only wish that it was Coalson he was taking the field against, instead of Thawley, for he was certain that Coalson was behind the entire thing.

"Gentlemen," Doakes said, "if there can be no compromise reached, I must ask that you each withdraw so that your seconds may examine and choose weapons."

Denholm eyed the temporary table that had been set up nearby, then moved off the required number of paces. Mylin knew his preference and would make the final decision after reviewing what had been assembled on the table. Normally, back in the Core, Denholm would have simply stated his weapon preference, but dueling sets hadn't been high on anyone's list of things to bring to Dalthus, it seemed. Most had viewed the mass on the transport ships more usefully used on chickens.

As a result, the table was filled with a hodgepodge of options collected from the other colonists. Blades, none of them matched unless by happenstance and all intended for some other, more mundane purpose, and a variety of firearms equally mismatched.

He'd had a difficult time telling Mylin what to choose for him, given that. All of the choices were far more utilitarian and deadly than would be used for a typical duel back in the Core. Finesse was difficult with a machete, after all, and firearms and lasers designed for dueling sets were less accurate by design than those the colonists had brought with them.

Most of the colonists. Denholm eyed the table again from his new place. There were two proper dueling cases on it, both supplied by the same man. *And sure it would be Rashae Coalson who's used his shipping space for those instead of something useful.*

Denholm watched Mylin look the things over, then nod at one of Coalson's cases. He frowned as Doakes picked up the case and walked toward him with Coalson and Mylin. He'd have thought they'd go to Thawley first.

He'd suspected that's what he'd wind up with — anything from the hodgepodge of weapons collected from the other colonists was too variable for him and he didn't trust the pair of antique pistols Coalson had provided not to have some trick to them.

Likely these do too, he thought, eyeing the thin swords in the case Doakes held.

"It's a bit off protocol," Mylin said as the three arrived near Denholm, "but we're agreed you're to choose first."

Coalson snorted.

"Mister Coalson, it's only fair," Doakes said. "What with you supplying the weapons and having a principal upon the field. We'd not want our colony's first days marred with whispers of impropriety, would we?"

"Shouldn't have accepted a challenge if he couldn't supply the weapons of his choice," Coalson said.

"Saw blades at twenty paces, Rashae?" Denholm asked. "Plows to first blood? You're the only one of us who spent shipping credits on what can only be used to kill your neighbors."

"Gentlemen!" Doakes stepped between them. "A principal and the other's second may not speak! It is unseemly." He turned his back to Coalson and held out the box to Denholm, speaking formally. "As challenged party, sir, the letter of the code does dictate that you should bring a set of weapons or agree that each of you will supply his own, but with so few available, and with these having been supplied by your opponent's second, I have agreed it's only proper you should pick from them first."

Denholm nodded. The blades were identical, long and thin with basket hilts. He'd prefer them, despite their having come from Coalson, as being least damaging.

Unless Thawley insists his honor won't be satisfied by a simple pinking.

Denholm chose one of the swords, tested its balance, and swished it through the air a couple times. It was a bit heavier in the hilt than he'd prefer, but he nodded to Doakes. The three men turned without a word and went over to Thawley.

"Gentlemen, I will ask once more," Doakes called once Thawley was armed. "Can honor not be satisfied in some other way this morning?"

"It cannot," Thawley called out.

"Mister Thawley, as the offended party the conditions are yours to name." Doakes nodded toward the watching crowd. "I will simply say that we are a very young colony and that tones are set by events like these. One should consider the —"

"Enough, Doakes!" Coalson yelled. "Do your bloody job and no more, will you? The man knows what his honor demands, it's not your place to lecture him!"

Denholm watched Thawley throughout. The other man seemed to be growing more nervous and hesitant, and kept glancing from Coalson to the crowd of watchers and back again.

For himself, Denholm felt oddly calm. He might be dead in another few minutes, but worrying at it wouldn't help. He was confident in his own abilities, even with an unfamiliar weapon. Though he'd never fought a serious duel, there'd been mocks and minor passes to first blood at school. Even with those, though, there was a risk of serious injury and the better man didn't always win. Once blades were crossed, any number of things could happen.

Thawley looked from Coalson to the crowd again and firmed his shoulders.

"First blood," he said. "The insult was not so grave."

Denholm glanced at Coalson, who reddened visibly.

So you told your cat's paw to go for more, did you? But can't very well dress him down for it after speaking so to Doakes?

Doakes nodded. He moved to the center of the space between them.

"Crossed or as you stand, Mister Carew?" Doakes asked.

"As we stand," Denholm said. He wanted the space between them at the start, wanted to see Thawley coming and how he moved and held his blade.

"Very well." Doakes gestured for Coalson and Mylin to step back with him. When they were a few meters removed from the combatants, he took a deep breath. "Begin."

DENHOLM WATCHED THAWLEY APPROACH WARILY.

He was more than a bit surprised at the man, as he'd expected Thawley to rush right at him. Instead he was circling and moving slowly, drawing nearer, but taking his time about it.

Denholm took the time to size him up as best he could.

He moved lightly on his feet, something else that surprised Denholm, and his sword was held loosely, wrist flexing, tip dancing about to draw the eye.

Denholm frowned.

Perhaps Thawley wasn't as inexperienced or nervous as he'd first assumed. The man seemed to have some skill.

Thawley came closer, not within range where their blades could touch, but close enough that Denholm didn't want to stand still and let him come. He turned and edged away slightly, Thawley following his movements closely, and the two began circling, just out of reach.

Thawley lunged, blade tip leaping forward, body turned to offer the least target possible.

Denholm reacted just as quickly, his counter determined not so much by conscious thought as a natural reaction to Thawley's technique. Thawley's school seemed to have taught him a bit of finesse — Denholm's alma mater had taught that as well, but they'd also taught their students to stay alive. As one of Denholm's more cynical peers at school had put it, "We can't very well respond to their donation requests from a box underground, now can we?"

Denholm deflected Thawley's blade to his left, wrist high, blade pointed down. Thawley began to recover, pulling back, but Denholm moved into him, keeping his blade in contact, spinning counterclockwise and raising his left elbow for a strike at Thawley's head.

Thawley moved away from the blow, but it had been a feint on Denholm's part. Instead he flung his right elbow up. It meant his blade blocked Thawley's closer to the tip, where he had less leverage, and risked a slicing cut as Thawley withdrew, but Thawley wasn't expecting that. The force of Denholm's arm drove his elbow into Thawley's face, which was moving in the opposite direction to avoid the feint and added to the impact.

Thawley staggered back, blood spurting from his nose.

Denholm stepped back and lowered his blade.

"First blood," he said.

"From a blade, damn your eyes!" Coalson yelled.

Thawley was still staggering backward, hunched over, hands to his face and blade barely in his grasp.

"First blood," Denholm repeated, then turned his attention back to Thawley. "If it satisfies, Mister Thawley?"

Thawley looked up at him, eyes watery and blinking. Blood covered the lower half of his face and his mouth was full of it, he had to spit twice before he could speak.

"Aye," he said. "It satisfies." He straightened, spat again, then glared first at Denholm and finally at Coalson. He flung his sword to the ground. "It's enough." He turned and strode away.

NINE

"Damn me, but this won't ..."

Denholm pulled the bolt from its place and looked from it to the nut in his other hand. It was difficult to tell in the shadowy, cramped space underneath the wagon, so he set the two together and tried to turn the nut. Clearly the wrong size.

"Well, then ..."

He reached the hand with the bolt out from beneath the wagon where he lay and called out, "Lynelle! Is there a nut left in the pack that will fit this?" He waved it back and forth. "Lynelle?"

"Well and will wagging it to and fro at me do a thing for you, do you think, love?"

Denholm felt her take the bolt.

"I'm sorry — this bloody thing has my temper short." He studied the underside of the wagon where there was just the single bolt left to install, if the thing's instructions were to be believed. "And there's a bit or two I'd rather be wagging at you, truth be told."

"Hmph." Lynelle handed him the bolt with a new nut already threaded on it to show that it fit. "The shelter's packed and I'll want more than a tent with this crowd around, afore there's any wagging to be done."

Denholm installed the bolt and started tightening it.

"Only for the one night; then we'll be on our way."

"And not a bit too soon for me, afore there's more trouble frae that bawjaws, Coalson, an' his crowd."

Denholm grunted agreement as he slid the bolt home and began tightening it in place.

"Denholm! Love! The shuttles're leavin', I think!"

He gave one last tug at the wrench to be certain the nut was well-tightened and slid out from beneath the wagon. Lynelle was staring past the lines of tents toward the vast open plain they'd chosen for their landing site on Dalthus. The commotion he'd grown used to in the three days since they'd first made planetfall had quieted and the crowds of people were all still and staring in the same direction.

As the next silver shape lifted silently above the tents, turned to orient itself with whichever ship it had come from, and then acceler-ated out of sight, Denholm wrapped his arms around Lynelle from behind and rested his chin on her head.

"Well and truly on our own," he whispered. Another of the shut-tles lifted, then another, and soon the rest, leaving the plain empty, with only the impressions on the grass to show that there was a universe at all outside of those settlers on the plain. "Six or more months before they return with the rest of the supplies and the first of the indentures."

Lynelle shivered and turned to face him. "I'm glad we're to be so close to Landing, love. Not like some."

Many of the colonists had chosen to land together and build their first homesteads near Landing, but some, the Coalsons included, much to Denholm's delight, had decided to make their first, and main, steadings farther away — the colony's antigrav hauler and the ships' boats had been busy ferrying them about the planet this whole time.

Denholm and Lynelle had chosen a river plain a bit over forty kilometers from the landing site and to not have their goods delivered there directly.

Their selected plain backed up to the *varrenwood*-covered hills they shared with the Mylin family. The Mylins had chosen to build their home on the other side of those hills and the surveys of the land suggested it would be less than a day's ride through the hills between the two farmsteads. Both families had chosen to have their goods unloaded at Landing and to make the trek to their new homes themselves. Denholm felt it would be best to get the lay of the land on that journey from the landing site, so that they'd have at least seen what they'd have to travel over to return. Though the colony had detailed aerial surveys from the colonial survey ships and had brought a small constellation of communication and positioning satellites, the map was not the land itself.

"Closer if Mylin had got that bit of marshland to drive a causeway through, instead of Coalson snapping it up for spite and denying us rights to build."

"Hush," Lynelle said. "Nae more aboot that man — he's put his home on the coast, far from us and ours. At least fer ..." She stopped speaking and Denholm felt her shiver.

"I've a feeling it's not over between us, even now." He shrugged. "Nothing for it, though." He bent to kiss her. "The rest of the day loading, the celebration tonight, and on our way in the morning."

Lynelle nodded, face pressed tightly to him.

"Denholm?"

"Aye?"

She patted his chest. "You load the pigs, love."

———

"WELL THIS IS IT, THEN."

Denholm grasped Mylin's hand firmly and nodded. "Until one of us is bored enough to blaze a trail over the hills."

They were some ten kilometers outside of Landing, just short of the marsh the hills between their steadings drained into, and they'd have to part ways here to each have the easiest route to their destinations. Even if the marsh hadn't been taken by Coalson, and both of them had a distaste for the land itself just by association with the man, it wasn't terrain they were comfortable taking the horses and cattle over without a road. Even the wagons, weight offset to a degree by their tiny antigrav generators, would risk being bogged down.

Mylin looked over to where Lynelle and his wife, Elora, were hugging in a tearful goodbye of their own.

"I've a thought one of us'll be sent to blaze that trail soon," he said.

Denholm laughed. "Likely, yes." He clapped Mylin on the arm and stepped back. "At least that's the excuse we'll have, aye?"

"Come on then, El!" Mylin called, walking toward his wagons. "It's you set the schedule!"

Elora hugged Lynelle again and stepped toward her own wagons. "I'll wait no longer than I must for walls and a bed, Sewell!" she called out. "And you'll wait for other things so long as I must!"

Mylin flushed and shrugged to Denholm who covered his mouth with his hand.

Lynelle came to his side and they watched the wagon with the other couple and their children move away.

"Just the two of us now, love."

Denholm nodded. Perhaps he'd been too busy with assembling and loading the wagons, but he hadn't felt the sense of isolation others had described at the celebration the night before. Someone had built a bonfire on the landing plain and sparks floated up into the night sky mimicking the flight of the shuttles earlier in the day. The sight had driven many of the colonists to melancholy speeches about being alone on a new world. Others had breached whatever limited supplies of beer or spirits they'd stocked in their supplies and become either quiet or boisterous as their natures dictated.

Denholm and Lynelle had retired to their tent early and were off with the Mylins well before dawn. Chickens, ducks, and pigs, distressed by the predawn movement of their cages hanging from the wagons drew sleepy complaints from the occupants of the tents they passed. The wagons might resemble in basic design those Denholm had read ancient, planetbound holders had used to travel to their claims, but were quite different in several important ways.

The materials, for one, were more advanced, with these made out of strong, lightweight plastics. Each of Denholm's two wagons had a small electric motor to help the rear wheels along, powered by the solar collectors that made up the canopies. Once they arrived at their homestead, the wagons would be partially disassembled, becoming two much smaller wagons for use around the farm, along with more he could assemble with local woods and modern fittings they'd brought along. The solar collecting canopies would become a part of their home's dome, along with one of the motors to drive a water pump. The motors, along with the small antigrav generators, allowed the pair of horses attached to each wagon to pull the eight tons of supplies each carried.

"Aye, just the two of us."

TEN

Denholm slid the door to the domed shelter open and eased inside. He wasn't quite ready to call it a homestead, but work was progressing. Slowly, as there was so much other work to do, not least of which was enough fields planted so they'd be able to harvest a crop before the planet's winter set in. He'd brought enough supplies to last them a full year, though they'd be heartily tired of bread, rice, and beans by the end of it if this first harvest failed. Everything ached and he was quite certain that his muscles had spawned yet new muscles to pain and punish him more for what he'd just put them through.

The horses pull the bloody plow — how can it hurt so much?

"Boots!" Lynelle called from the kitchen area. "And wash up afore y'go an' sit yerself."

Denholm groaned. He wanted nothing more than to slip into a chair and have a plate full of whatever Lynelle was cooking. It smelled wonderful, and his stomach clenched with need to be filled.

"Boots and bath!" Lynelle called.

He slipped his boots off near the door and made his way to the bath compartment, the only enclosed space in the dome. Other than that it had a living area which converted to a bedroom, and a small kitchen area. He had to admit, though, that the hot water felt wonderful.

He made a mental note to check the supply of flexible piping to ensure he had enough to irrigate the field he'd just plowed. He'd thought four rolls of the thin, flat hose would be sufficient, but, as with virtually everything in their supplies, he'd quickly found himself wishing for more. They'd placed the shelter far enough from the river to avoid what appeared to be the most common flooding, so there was the piping run from river to shelter, then from the shelter to the second, larger dome that made up the barn. More for the small garden near the domes and finally to the fields, the first of which he'd just plowed.

Soon he'd have a waterwheel built upstream to deliver water via aqueduct to cisterns near the homestead and fields, freeing up the pump and motor for other uses.

Soon, aye. And one day replace that wheel with a pump built here on Dalthus.

It was a cycle he knew he'd see throughout the farm. Use the expensive, unsupportable technology they'd brought with them for the most critical tasks, until a primitive solution could be formed, then replace that again and again as what could be fabricated on-planet improved.

We'll watch the whole history of more than one device play out before our eyes here.

No matter the warnings they'd received before leaving New London, the amount of work and how long it took still came as a surprise. He let the hot water ease yet another ache he hadn't been aware of and thought about the tasks he'd just completed. Part of the reason for doing that was to ensure he'd done everything, though he had a checklist on his tablet to help him. Just caring for the plow team and equipment, then seeing that the rest of the stock, including the chickens and pigs, was safely in the barn took so much time. Seeing to it that they had feed and water to last the night. Double-checking the chickens' roost was doubly important, for there was a smallish native predator that had developed a taste for terrestrial fowl, despite it being indigestible to them.

Thought of the native species made him wince and ease his leg. Three days before he'd learned to walk the field he planned to plow beforehand, striking the ground ahead with a long stick. The lesson had come from plowing over a nest of some sort of insect that resembled a wasp. The stings from those were painful, but not dangerous he'd been glad to find, once he'd hurriedly taken a sample with his tablet and waited for the doctor in Landing to analyze the data.

He used a bit more of the valuable soap to finish washing and rinsed himself, dried himself and dressed in fresh clothes. Even clean clothing was to be rationed when washing meant stirring them by hand in a great pot of hot water and hanging them to dry. Lynelle had brought the first bit of washing in and promptly divided Denholm's clothing into three sets.

"These're fer fields and these fer at-home an' these fer go-to-town, love," she'd said. "An' if ever the *tri* meet, it'll gae poorly for you."

The smell of dinner on the table made his mouth water as he left the bathing compartment, but he took the time to check that the monitor was turned on and working properly. The little device perched atop the dome's windmill would scan the surrounding area for motion or heat and alert him if anything approached. He also checked the laser rifle he kept by the shelter's door. Both the loaded capacitor and the spare read as fully-charged, which would give him a dozen shots between them — more than enough if the creature he couldn't help but call a weasel came after the chickens. Perhaps enough if the hulking, shuffling shape Sewall Mylin had reported seeing up in the hills on his property proved to be real. With some new species it wasn't so simple a matter of hitting them with the shot as it was finding the spot that would be fatal and not simply irritating.

Denholm eased himself into a seat at the table. He winced as the weight came off the leg that had been stung and the pain he'd become used to during the day eased. He closed his eyes and sighed, keeping them closed until he heard the click of a plate on the table before him and hands begin to knead his shoulders.

"A hard day, then?" Lynelle asked.

Denholm groaned as her hands continued to work on his shoulders. "No harder than the one before, nor tomorrow. And yours?"

Lynelle slid her arms around him from behind and held her hands up in front of him. The tips of her fingers were red and worn.

"I hope y'find the chicken on yer plate tasty, love, for the plucking's a chore, it is."

"Chicken?" Denholm looked down in surprise. He'd not seen meat on a plate for weeks. No wonder his stomach had reacted so to the smell of it cooking.

"She weren't laying, and I'll have no freeloaders in my farmyard." Lynelle took her own seat. "Is the plowing finished, as ye'd hoped?"

Denholm nodded, mouth full of chicken and gravy. He swallowed and used a biscuit — a bit burnt on the bottom, but he'd neither mention it nor care — to sop up the juices. The chicken was as much celebration as they'd allow themselves for finishing the plowing, and he'd not waste a bit of calories or flavor. Rice, beans, and nutrition bars which had made the trip to Dalthus stuffed into the ship's hold had grown old and tiresome long ago.

"Tomorrow's the slurry, and it'll take both of us for that."

Lynelle nodded, her own mouth full.

Now that he'd plowed the land, the next step was to lay down the slurry, a concentrated mix of terrestrial nutrients, bacteria, and insect larvae shipped out in dense, meter-sized cubes. They'd only need one of the cubes, dissolved in water, to treat the land he'd cleared so far, but a week after treatment the land would be able to support their crops as the terrestrial bugs took over and drove out anything local. The rest of the cubes would go to treat other fields, both the additional home fields for the indentures, who'd be arriving in a few months. More of those cubes would arrive with the indentures for use on the eventual commercial fields for export crops.

Once these first fields were planted, though, he could begin to concentrate on other things. All the other things that seemed to multiply with every passing day.

"It's deathly sick o' potatoes, we'll be," Lynelle said between mouthfuls. "One wonders if the indentures e'en know what it is they're in for."

"Aye."

Potatoes and sweet potatoes were the first crops — hardy and nutrient rich. Lynelle was starting a house garden for some variety, and the indentures would as well, but until the second year's crops came in with something more than root vegetables, they'd all be mightily tired of the sameness of it. But their calorie content meant less land to plow and their hardiness meant more time for those other tasks, so they'd have to suffer through.

Start a road ... path, really, toward those hills and meet up with Mylin. Get samples of that varrenwood off on the ships that bring the indentures — that'll be our first real export for cash, and the quickest to see a return. Scout out the locations for the first commercial fields.

He sighed.

And that all with seeing that our first crops don't fail and we all starve next year.

ELEVEN

Denholm ran his eyes up the trunk of the tree. It was two meters across at the base and nearly a hundred meters high.

And this is a small one, he thought, pulling the laser cutter from the wagon.

The mature *varrenwoods* could measure twenty meters at the base. Not much higher, though. The trees grew upward quickly in their youth, racing for the scarce breaks in the canopies of the older trees and spreading their branches at the top to force out competition. The clearing this one had sprouted in was the result of one of those massive trees falling to clear both its canopy space and that of the others its fall took down.

Sewall Mylin had found the clearing and brought it to Denholm's attention. It was situated on a saddleback that would make an easy route over the hills between the two properties and they'd decided to place their first small mill at the site. Not a large one, just enough to prepare the logs for transport to Landing by antigrav hauler or trim them to manageable size for dragging back to the homesteads. A second, larger mill would be sited once they had the beginnings of a road from their holdings to Landing.

Denholm smiled at the thought of their new buildings being made entirely of a wood those on New London would pay a fortune for, even as a veneer.

The site for the mill was already laid out, with posts and string marking the corners and walls. They'd cleared a bit of the brush together, but they'd have to wait until the first round of indentures arrived in a week's time to raise the building. Denholm had solar panels arriving on those ships as well, which would go to power the mill and charge the laser cutters on site.

This tree, though, was in the way, and cut into manageable chunks and dragged the ten kilometers back to the homestead, would become the boards the new indentures would use to build their bunkhouses. Until then they'd be housed in the large tents also arriving.

Denholm keyed the laser cutter on, spared one last glance down the slope to be sure of where he wanted to lay the tree, and began cutting. *Varrenwood* had an oddly pleasant scent when it burned; almost like vanilla but with a hint more spice. The cutter made short work of the tree's thick, knobby bark, exposing the cream-colored wood beneath. That cream was shot through with pockets of dark purple sap, the distinctive pattern and coloring that Denholm hoped would make *varrenwood* a very profitable export.

He notched the trunk then moved to the back and cut almost through. The remaining ten percent or so of the trunk would act as a hinge and send the tree down in the direction of the notch. He turned off the laser cutter and took up a wedge and mallet to send the tree on its way.

There was a rustling sound and one of the horses picketed near the wagon neighed loudly.

Denholm froze. The sound came again and now both horses were alarmed, jerking against their halters and stamping their feet. The wagon and horses were fifty meters down the slope and to one side of Denholm.

The horses screamed and tried to rear and then Denholm could see what they did coming around a tree trunk only ten meters from the wagon. It looked exactly as Mylin had described it after his own brief glimpse of the beast. More than three meters long and two at the shoulder, thick, dense fur that was mottled almost like camouflage, wide, heavy paws tipped with claws, and a muzzle full of teeth.

Aye, the unnatural offspring of a grizzly and a puma, as Mylin said.

The horses screamed again and the beast moved, faster than Denholm thought possible for something so large. It was on the horses in an instant, felling one with a blow from its paw and taking the other's neck between its jaws.

Denholm took a cautious step back, hoping to get behind the *varrenwood* trunk and out of the beast's sight. His rifle was on the wagon and he cursed himself for leaving it there and not having it to hand. He had a flechette pistol on his hip, better suited to small vermin than the massive beast.

Three hundred kilos, maybe more.

The laser cutter would make short work of anything it touched, but that would mean getting within reach of those claws. Not an event Denholm thought he'd long survive.

If he could get out of sight, then perhaps the beast would eat its fill of the horses — a loss Denholm felt dearly, but not worth his life — and be on its way. He took another step backward. Something cracked underfoot and the beast raised its head, muzzle red and dripping. It cocked its head, caught sight of Denholm, and spun to face him.

Denholm grasped the butt of his flechette pistol, but eyeing the beast's mass he didn't think he'd be able to bring it down before it reached him. Even if the beast reached him as nothing but dead weight he'd be in for a bad time. Running was out of the question, as fast as he'd seen it move.

The beast surged toward him, and Denholm, without conscious thought, began scrabbling up the *varrenwood's* trunk. The bark was knobby and coarse, with deep fissures that gave him hand and footholds. He was five meters up before he was really even aware of where he placed his hands and feet at all, and still moving upward.

One of his footholds crumbled beneath him and he dropped to hang by his hands, feet seeking another hold. There was a roar and he looked down to find the beast on its hind legs against the tree, paws stretched upward and bare centimeters from his feet.

Denholm's body seemed to move on its own accord and he was several meters higher before he paused, breathless, and looked down again.

The beast was back on all fours, shuffling around the base of the tree and occasionally looking up at Denholm.

Bearcat? If I'm to be the first one eaten by the beastie, do I at least get to name it? No, bearcat's a silly name — I'll not be eaten by something named that.

The thing paused in its circling of the trunk and went up on its hind legs again. It clawed at the trunk once, twice, then flexed its hind legs and hopped onto the trunk. Its claws dug at the bark and it began moving upward in a hitching, jerky gait a few centimeters at a time.

"The bloody thing can *climb?*" Denholm began inching higher himself. "Look, you! There's a thousand kilos of horseflesh there for the taking, what do you want with me?" He made sure his grip on the trunk was solid and let go with one hand to draw his flechette pistol. "You can't even digest me, damn you!"

Aiming was difficult, being down the trunk, but he managed a shot that sent darts into the beast's paw. It let loose with a howl of pain and fell to the ground, rolling down the slope away from the tree.

Denholm took aim again as it got to its feet, gnawing at the paw riddled with darts. His next shot took it in the shoulder and the beast went to its hind legs, roared in anger, and rushed the tree.

"Oh, hell," Denholm muttered, nearly dropping the flechette pistol as the massive tree shook from the impact.

Denholm fired again, but missed. He began climbing higher to gain more distance before his next shot, but the beast was eeling its way up the tree faster than before, as though anger at being shot was fueling it. Denholm's next shot hit it, but it simply paused, roared, and resumed its climb. Denholm climbed higher as well.

He reached up to find a new handhold and felt the entire tree shift, forcing him to clutch the rough bark desperately.

The tree jerked again as the beast continued to climb.

He'd cut through most of the trunk at the base, leaving only a bit of it to act as a hinge, but the tree had been stable, resting on that thin cut. Now, though, with hundreds of kilos climbing higher on the downhill side, the side with the notch cut, that solid hinge of wood was giving way.

There was a loud *crack*, from below, the tree jerked and a second, louder *crack* sounded.

Denholm looked down. The beast had stopped climbing as well and Denholm wondered if it was smart enough to realize what was happening.

The tree tilted downslope a bit, another *crack* sounded, and it tilted more, then there was a roar of tearing wood and the massive trunk began to tumble.

Denholm scrambled around the trunk to the uphill side and had barely a moment to wonder whether it would be best to ride it down or try to leap off at the last moment, and then it was too late to think.

TWELVE

Denholm opened his eyes to pain, cold, and a star-filled sky. Which, given the alternative, he thought he should be quite happy about. Then he rolled to his side and the blinding pain that shot through him gave him pause to reconsider.

No ... no, still better the pain than the alternative.

He lay still for a moment, testing his muscles and feeling out his body. Everything hurt, it seemed, but particularly his left side. He could wiggle his toes, and that was a good sign, but moving his left leg was a very bad thing indeed — the same with his left arm. He thought something might be broken in each of them. He ran his right hand over himself and quickly found the break in his left forearm. His ribs were tender, but didn't seem broken, and his left hip appeared unhurt. He couldn't reach the pain in his lower left leg to check it, he quickly found. Any attempt to sit up or raise his head sent waves of nausea through him.

That would be the thing of most concern, he decided, how badly he'd struck his head.

He tried again to sit up, keeping his left arm tucked close to him and gritting his teeth against the pain and nausea.

This time he made it. He rested for a moment, propping himself up with his right arm, until the feelings faded and he could move again.

The light from the stars and Dalthus' two moons gave some light in the clearing, enough for Denholm to take stock of his situation. If he'd been under the forest's thick canopy it would be totally dark. He was midway down the slope, but on the opposite side of the fallen *varrenwood* from the wagon. He shifted so he could see both up and down the slope, wincing as pain shot up his leg.

It was possibly the worst place he could have landed, short of directly underneath the *varrenwood* itself, of course. It was fifty or more meters up or down the slope to get around the *varrenwood's* trunk, then that same distance up or down the slope to get to the wagon. Both ways were difficult and he had no way of knowing what state the other side of the slope was in, but he had to manage it. He had to get to the wagon. The wagon held his food, his water, and the tablet that would connect to the satellites and let him call for help. The wagon meant life.

Lynelle would be worried that he hadn't arrived home before dark and hadn't used his tablet to call her, but she wouldn't have noted that until after dark and would wait until morning before coming to look for him. The path up into the hills was too rough to risk a horse on in the dark — he'd needed the antigrav generators from both wagons installed on the one he'd brought up here. If he could get to the tablet and call her, they could call for an antigrav hauler to fly him to Landing and medical attention. He wasn't too worried about the broken bones, those could be repaired, but he was concerned about injuries he couldn't sense — whether internal or his head.

He started up the slope, right hand and right foot working to drag himself over the rough ground. Up would be better to start, he thought, now when he had the most strength, then the downhill slope to finish it.

Fifty meters up, fifty meters down ... call it five meters to get to the

other side of the trunk where it's clear. A hundred and five meters,
more or less.

He planted his right hand and pushed with his foot, dragging
himself a few more centimeters up the slope. The broken arm was not
so bad as the broken leg — with every bit of movement, his foot
dragged on the ground, pulling at the break.

Ten centimeters at a time ... bloody hell ... twenty-one hundred
or more ...

Again he planted his hand to brace himself and pushed himself
up the slope, crying out at the pain.

"*Three!* You motherless bastard!"

And again.

"*Four!* Bloody bearcat's too good a name for you! *Five!* It's shite-
weasel for you! *Six!* I'll look up the bloody Latin for that!"

He had to pause, arm trembling and he'd broken out in a sweat
that had gone clammy in the night air.

"*Seven!* Keep your bloody rifle in bloody arm's reach, you bloody
fool!"

By the time he was halfway up the slope, his arm was trembling,
barely able to lift him off the ground for the little bit of ground he
gained, and he'd stopped counting.

Silly thing to start anyway.

The bones in his leg ground together with every movement and
he realized that he couldn't feel his left foot anymore, but he
clenched his jaw and kept going. Any damage short of it actually
falling off could likely be repaired with the medical equipment in
Landing, he only needed to get there alive.

The horses ... damn.

Half their carting stock gone in an instant, and the other two
were with foal. That one loss would cost them half the funds they'd
kept in reserve — they'd have to buy two new carting horses when the
next ships arrived. Unless he could find someone on-planet who'd
part with a pair for less, and that was unlikely.

He reached the stump of the fallen tree and edged around it, then paused. He rested his back against the stump and closed his eyes.

Just for a moment, I'll rest.

It was past dawn when he opened them again. He couldn't tell how far past, but he cursed himself for falling asleep. The numbness in his leg frightened him. If the circulation had been cut off and it went too long, they might not be able to repair the damage in Landing. It wouldn't be the end of him, he could get a prosthetic, but that would be even more cost to order and ship the thing. Worse, he felt hot — more so than the morning sun could account for. Either the chill and damp of the night or his injuries had left him feverish, and that wasn't a good sign either way.

He started down the slope and realized that this was harder than going up. He had to go down backwards, so that his injured leg would drag instead of bunching up, and the angle was awkward. He considered standing and hopping, but the ground was too rough and he felt too weak and lightheaded. Bit by bit he made his way down the slope.

His palm landed on something wet and sticky. That startled him and he jerked it back, crying out from the pain the movement sent through him. He eased himself a bit and looked at what he'd put his hand in.

The beast hadn't made it from under the *varrenwood* during the fall and had been crushed. He'd crawled into a pool of blood and viscera seeping out from beneath the tree.

"I'll make a rug of you," Denholm promised the carcass. "A shite-weasel rug, and my family'll wipe their feet on you for generations."

He closed his eyes, trying to calm his breathing. The wagon was within sight — almost within reach. Just another few meters. His arm gave out and he was suddenly flat on his back, head pointed down the slope. He knew he should go on — had to reach the wagon. For water, for the tablet that would call help. But he was so tired and it felt so good to close his eyes and rest again for just a moment.

The sun was higher when he woke, warm on his skin, but he still found himself shivering. He judged the time from the slant of light through the forest canopy and took stock of his situation. He might make it after all — Lynelle would arrive soon if she'd left the homestead at dawn and he was certain she would have.

He shifted his shoulders, they were stiff and aching, then froze. He'd heard something.

He kept still, listening, and the sound came again. A snuffling exhale. He cracked his eyes open.

Oh ... hell.

No more than three meters away was another of those damn beasts. It was hunched over the carcass of the first one, sniffing.

A mate? Or some other sort of pairing?

Not that it mattered. What mattered was that it was so close and Denholm had nothing to defend himself with. Even the flechette pistol, not that it would do any good, was lost somewhere on the other side of the *varrenwood*.

Denholm stayed still, trying to go unnoticed.

Smell your bloody friend, then go eat your fill of some nice horses and go away.

The snuffling grew closer. Even with his eyes closed Denholm could feel the beast come nearer, still it was only with an effort of will that he kept himself from jumping when a great nose nudged the side of his head. Air moved over his head and neck as the beast sniffed at him. There was a large rock under his right hand — he thought he might be able to grasp and lift it, but what then? He couldn't prop himself up on his broken left arm to gain any leverage for a swing.

Better than going quietly to his dinner plate.

"Denholm!"

The call came from far away, down the slope along the path he'd used to bring the wagon up, but it was loud enough that the beast stopped sniffing at him and raised its head. Lynelle had come and knew nothing of the beasts. Denholm's fingers tightened around the rock.

"Denholm!"

The beast snorted and shuffled away, farther down the slope.

Denholm opened his eyes and saw it halfway between him and the wagon. Too far away to swing the rock — too far even to throw it if it was to be at all effective. Lynelle was closer now, he could see movement through the brush behind the wagon.

"Denholm, love! Are ye there? Call out!"

"Lynelle! *Run!*"

He grasped the rock and leveraged himself up, spinning so that he faced down the slope. The movement sent waves of pain through his leg and arm, and his leg bent at a disturbing angle. Facing downslope he was able to remain upright and raised the rock to throw.

"*Run!*"

"Denholm, where are ye?"

The beast was casting its head back and forth between the two sounds, as though unable to decide which was the greater threat — or perhaps which might be tastiest. It snarled and began bouncing on its forepaws in agitation.

Denholm threw the rock just as Lynelle, leading her horse, came up the path into sight of the wagon and the half-eaten carcasses of the cart horses. The rock bounced off the beast's hindquarter, but was ignored. The beast was fixated on Lynelle now, or perhaps her horse, which was larger and whinnying distress.

The beast started down the slope, deceptively fast for its size.

"*Run!*" Denholm cried. It was all he could think to do as he watched, helpless.

Lynelle dropped her horse's reins, which immediately spun and bolted down the path. She was carrying a rifle, one of the simpler, chemical propellant ones. She dashed toward the wagon, and its meager cover.

Denholm searched the ground around him for another rock as the beast rushed down the slope and Lynelle raised the rifle to her shoulder. His world narrowed to the sound of the beast's roaring as it charged, punctuated by the sharp *cracks* of Lynelle's rifle firing. He thought he shouted again, hoping to draw the beast's attention back, but perhaps he only screamed.

The beast staggered once, then struck the wagon, knocking it aside and blocking Denholm's view of Lynelle.

Three more *cracks* sounded, close together, and the beast sank to the ground.

"*Lynelle!*" Denholm got his right leg under him and tried to stand, but pain in his broken leg sent him back to the ground. "*Lynelle!*"

"Aye, love." She sounded out of breath. "A moment, then." There were two more shots and Lynelle rounded the far corner of the wagon, rifle to her shoulder and still trained on the creature.

Denholm closed his eyes and sank back.

In a moment Lynelle was beside him. He could hear her calling for help on her tablet, arranging for the colony's single antigrav hauler to come for him and winced at the cost. Still he didn't object — he could tell well enough that he needed to get to the medical facilities in Landing as quickly as possible.

"You're a right mess, love." Lynelle smoothed the hair back from his forehead.

"I told you to run," Denholm whispered.

"Aye, and I did, love. Straight to that wagon for a steadier shot."

"I meant *away*." Even to his ears his voice sounded petulant, but he found himself drifting and unable to focus. He opened his eyes and saw Lynelle adding a second patch to the one she'd already placed on his arm. He thought to tell her not to, that he could bear the pain and the drug patches from their medical kit were too dear to replace, but his mouth wouldn't form the words and his eyelids were so very heavy.

He felt her lips on his forehead.

"Aye, love, but y've got t'be specific with the Scots, you know? Thought you'd've learned that by now."

THIRTEEN

Denholm came awake grudgingly. His body ached, every bit of it, and the bed was so soft.

Awareness came back that, if he was in a bed, he couldn't also be in some shite-weasel's gullet, which let him remember the last events. Lynelle must have got him back to Landing and the doctor. He opened his eyes.

True enough, he was in a well-lit room in a well-made home. Bright sunshine shone through the white curtains over the window. The softness of the bed was matched by the softness of the comforter over him and the pillows beneath his head. For a moment, he closed his eyes again, thinking to go back to sleep for just a bit, but then there was movement in the room and a soft hand stroked his forehead.

"Awake, love?"

Denholm started to speak, but his throat was dry and he had to wait for Lynelle to ease a cup of water to his lips. He drank, swished a bit around his mouth, and swallowed.

"So I'm not dead, then?"

"No thanks to yourself, to be leavin' yer gun so far away," Lynelle said. She sat on the edge of the bed and took his hand. The one not bound to his chest beneath the bedclothes. "The arm'll heal fine and you'll ache for a time. Y'had a wee bug o' some sort to boot, but that's done." She hesitated. "The leg's the worst of it."

Denholm winced at the memory of things grinding together inside his leg.

"It was splintered bad, love, so y'ave eight centimeters and a bit o' printed bone t' replace it."

Denholm sighed. That was better than he'd feared, at least. His leg would ache with the weather, no getting around that, but eight centimeters of printed plastic grafted in there was better than losing the leg. The prosthetics the colony could produce were crude things and sending back to the Core for a modern one would be ruinously expensive.

"How long has it been? Who's watching the stock?" he asked, suddenly, realizing that with Lynelle there with him there'd be no one to take care of the homestead.

"Hush," Lynelle said, stroking his forehead again. "The Mylins' eldest is staying there to look after things, he's a steady lad."

Denholm nodded. Their neighbors' eldest lad was steady, not, perhaps, the brightest, though he'd never say that to Sewall or Elora, but he was a good, steady lad.

"How long?" he asked again.

"Almost a fortnight." Lynelle squeezed his hand. "The bug were a bad one, but they've a vaccine now the doctor's sent out to all the homesteads."

Denholm closed his eyes, weary. A fortnight would explain why he felt so weak, but to have been down so long would have other effects, as well.

"T' doctor's thinking that bug's tied to the bearcats," Lynelle continued. "A bit o' parasite that don't affect them but 'as a taste fer humans somehow."

"Bearcats?" Denholm frowned. "I told you to call them shite-weasels — I remember that, don't I?" Vague images of the ride from the logging camp to Landing were coming back. "I told someone ..."

Lynelle shook her head.

"No use, love. Once t'images o' that beastie went out, it were all bearcat." She paused. "Doctor Purdue did name the fever after you, though."

"What?"

"The Carew Ague ... has a bit o' a ring."

Denholm grimaced. "He didn't, really?"

Lynelle nodded. "Afraid so, love."

"The indentures?" he asked, wanting to change the subject.

"Still here in Landing," Lynelle said.

Denholm winced. That would mean more cost, housing and feeding them here in Landing for a week or more. That on top of the doctor's fees and the lost work.

"They seem ... acceptable," Lynelle continued.

Denholm shifted in the bed, easing himself more upright. His head spun for a moment, but then settled. Lynelle placed a hand on his chest.

"Lay back, love, yer still not fit."

"I need to see to the indentures," Denholm said, "and we need to get them back to the —"

He swung his legs off the bed and sat up, then the world spun and darkened.

"Ease back, now," Lynette said, "doctor said it's three days more he'll see you abed."

DENHOLM MANAGED to sit and even rise the next day, but it was the day after that before he had the strength to leave his room. Not the three days the doctor wanted, but more than Denholm could wish.

The indentures, those men and women who'd come to Dalthus to work, not as shareholders, on these later ships, were much as he'd expected. There were no criminals or debt-indentures in the first lot, that had been part of the settlers' contract with the shipping agency, just men and women looking for a fresh start but without the means to pay their own transport to a new system, much less buy shares in the colony.

Part of what he and Lynelle had paid for their shares would go toward the transport costs of the forty people who faced him now, having spent the last week since they'd left the transports in tents on a field near Landing instead of being moved along via the colony's hauler to their new homes.

What must they think of that? And of me?

Denholm wore a brace on his leg, and would for the next two weeks, as well as use a cane for two more after that, until the new bone was fully healed and he regained his strength.

He wondered what he should say to them.

"Welcome," he said. "I'm sorry I wasn't able to meet you when you landed." He gestured to his leg. "But it was break a few bones or be eaten, and I chose the former." He waited while the polite chuckles died down. "What happened to me should be a lesson to you, though. You're all here by choice and signed the charter — that you understand we're a new colony and the risks of that. The hardships."

He shook his head.

"You'll be mightily tired of potatoes and yams before this first year's through.

"It will be hard work. Harder than some of you have ever done, I know it's been so for me since we landed. But I promise you this. I'll be doing that work beside you and eating those potatoes with you — both of us," he continued, wrapping an arm around Lynelle's shoulder, "Lynelle and I."

"Together we'll make it through the first years, hard as they may be, and together we'll make something of this world that we can all be proud of. Something for ourselves and something for our families ... our children and our children's children, whenever they may come."

PART FOUR
DALTHUS IV

Planetfall plus 2.5 years

FOURTEEN

The farmhouse's kitchen was redolent with the scent of fresh cut wood — the particular, distinct scent of freshly cut *varrenwood,* as that was what most of room was built of. Floors, cabinets, walls, and the sturdy, rough-hewn table Denholm sat at all showed the peculiar grain of what had quickly become Dalthus' primary export back to the Core Worlds. The new farmhouse had gone up quickly once he felt he could spare the work of what never seemed to be enough hands from other tasks. It was small, tiny by Core World standards, but enough, Denholm thought, for the two of them for some time.

A kitchen and larder took up fully half the ground floor — it was amazing how much more space the simple preparation of food took without most modern devices — with dining and sitting rooms taking the rest. A pair of bedrooms and a bath upstairs completed the small house.

The sound of saws and hammers coming through the hazy panes of hand-poured glass in the window drew a small smile from him. The farm had grown in the two years since he'd brought the first indentured hands back from Landing, and they were busy at building a new barracks before the arrival of the next indenture ship at the colony — he'd be adding to his hands to work even more lands — and it amused him that those debtors and criminals would soon find themselves living in a building of wood those in the Core paid such ridiculous sums for.

More than the barracks, now, there was a small village starting in the bend of the river only a kilometer away. The population there was a combination of indentures with families and a few original colonists who had too few shares to take land of their own. Many of those had stayed in the original settlement after landing, but were now using their shares to start businesses near the more major holdings, betting on growth.

Denholm frowned as a half-heard rumble drew his attention from his tablet and the holding's accounts. The rumble grew gradually louder, but not so loud that it could drown out the shouts from outside. He set his tablet down and rose, making his way to the doorway.

A ship's boat was settling to the ground in the yard between house and the barracks buildings. Those working on the new barracks had set aside their tools to gather at the edge of the yard and stare at the new arrival.

"Denholm, love!" Lynelle's voice cut above the sound of the boat's engine as it settled to the ground, sending chickens scurrying for shelter. Denholm winced as she came around the house's corner, a bundle of linens she'd been retrieving from the wash lines over her arm. "It's twice I've asked ye to put down a pad for landing a distance from the house."

"Yes, the twice before one's landed here these two years past." He moved to meet her and took half the load to place on the house's porch. "That's a good bit of time and material to lay down for use once a year."

"It's you'll be keening complaints when there's no eggs these next mornings, what with the chickens terrified again."

Denholm took her half of the load to set down and kissed her cheek.

"I'll settle for a bit of bacon and make no complaint of it."

Lynelle poked him in the midriff, eliciting an *uf* of air.

"Bacon'll undo the benefits, love."

Denholm grimaced. He'd thought he was in decent physical shape when they'd left New London, but there was no doubt the two years since landing on Dalthus had had an effect. The never-ending hard work and limited diet had seen to it that they all, holder and indenture alike, had not a bit of extra fat by this time. The first six months after the indentures arrived had been the most difficult and they'd all, as Denholm had predicted, been heartily sick of potatoes and sweet potatoes, augmented by the supplies they'd brought with them, by the time the first grains and greens had been ready for harvest. A few months later the chicken population reached the point where Denholm felt they could spare more than a few eggs and even the occasional low producer for the indentures' pot.

Now the household and the indentures managed their own poultry separately and there were eggs aplenty along with a full bird every few days.

The pigs, on the other hand ...

"I'll have bacon before the year's out," Denholm said. "Regular and proper."

The pigs bred slower than the chickens, and Denholm, true to his word to the indentures, had restrained himself from indulging in anything he couldn't offer to them as well. But the holding's sounder of the animals had grown, and there were more than enough boars now, that he'd decided more than one of them would see the inside of a smokehouse come autumn. Then there'd be bacon and hams enough for the main house and barracks for the next year — and the autumn after might see enough for that and for a bit of profit in Land-ing, as well.

"As you say, love." Lynelle nodded to the boat, whose ramp was lowering. "Best see to the visitors."

Denholm nodded and started across the farmyard toward the boat.

They'd had word via the satellite constellation that a ship had arrived in system, but nothing about its nature or purpose. Dalthus was still too new to be on the agenda of many merchants not specifically contracted to deliver to the colony. There were few exports to speak of so far, other than the *varrenwood*. But some independent merchantmen stopped by to ply their wares. Of those, two others had sent boats to the Carew holding, but they'd had the courtesy to contact him first and ask his permission to set down on his lands.

This one had simply arrived, as though they had every right to set down in whichever farmyard they might choose. And it was a larger boat than he'd seen before, almost twenty meters in length, though ill-kept. One of the landing struts sagged, giving the boat a decided list to one side, and its flanks were oddly pocked and stained.

The rear ramp lowered and a dozen men emerged, no more well-kept than the boat itself. While Denholm wasn't expecting the well turned-out crew of a Naval vessel or a major shipper like the Marchant Company, he hadn't expected such a motley sight as this either. No two of the men seemed to be wearing the same color, much less style, of ship's jumpsuits, and one, Denholm assumed he was the ship's captain as he strode out to meet Denholm with a wide smile on his face, wore what looked to be a Naval captain's dress coat, somewhat torn and stained and with the gilt removed, over his.

"Oy, there, then!" the man called. "Are you the holder here?"

"I am," Denholm said, taking the man's hand once he was close enough.

"Maximillian Saint, captain of the *Vainglorious Rose*." He shook Denholm's hand vigorously. "The one aptly named, for she's a wallowing tub with no cause for pride, and the other not at all, for I'm bound to a warmer place, for certain, or so my suffering missus is prone to speechify upon."

Denholm blinked. "I see ... Captain Saint. Or, rather, I believe I do."

"Hope it was all right for us to set down there. Didn't see proper landing space, nor an unused field near."

"Here is quite all right for the number of visitors we get," Denholm said, ignoring the muffled *hmph* from Lynelle, "but I'm afraid it's a wasted landing for you if you've a mind to take on a cargo." He nodded toward the outbuildings and piles of lumber being used for the new barracks. "All we have for export is the *varrenwood* and the bit we have milled or logged is either spoken for in our own buildings or already under contract in Landing."

"That is a lovely wood — I can see it'd be desired back in the Core. To be picked up soon, is it?" Saint raised his eyebrows.

"Within a month or two. The wood is much in demand, so what we can mill is loaded quite regularly."

Saint looked around the farmstead, scanning things casually. "What ship's due, if I might ask? It's possible I know the man and would want to stay to meet him ..." He grinned. "Or owe him a bit of coin and would want to be away."

Denholm laughed.

"I don't rightly know the ship itself that's due next. One of the Marchant hulls, I suppose, as they're who I've contracted with to carry the lumber."

Saint's mouth twisted. "Marchant, yes. Well, they're a safe bet for your cargo, of course. Better armed and manned than most other lines or us independents." He frowned. "I do know a Marchant captain or two ... due in a month, you said?"

"Or more — it's hard to say. Again, I'm sorry if you've wasted a landing, as I've no cargo for you. In a year or so I hope to have hams available, but we've none now."

Saint smiled again. "Now a bit of ham would go well with the lads, I'll say, so I'll keep that in mind when next we're through this system. Truth to tell, though, we're not much for cargo, ourselves." He gestured toward the group of men — and women, Denholm now saw, though it was hard to tell in their grubby gear — assembled at the boat's ramp. "We're more of an ... independent band. I may be captain, but we've all a share in the ship and take our own cargoes.

Small crafts and such, a bit of odds and ends and this and thats. Amusements, as well, if you've a mind."

"Amusements?"

"Oh, yes," Saint said, grinning. "Bit of a traveling fair ... though we're no great showmen. No huge tents and such, just a few booths to ply wares and display a talent or two. Crandall, there —" He pointed toward the group, though Denholm couldn't tell to which man. "— has a crate of a peppered jam from Eidera. Some local fruit, perfectly edible and tasty." He paused. "There *is* a lad or two likes to run a game of chance, if you've a mind to allow it?"

Denholm looked around. He suspected those games of "chance" had more surety for the man running them than was strictly fair, but such was to be assumed with a group like this. Work on the new barracks had all but ceased and the crowd of men and women drew closer to the *Vainglorious Rose's* boat, and he could see expectant looks on their faces. A bit of a fair day wouldn't put the work off for any time that would be a harm, and life on the holding was so insular that new faces and news from out-system were always welcome.

"Your amusements would be most welcome, I think, Captain Saint. There's a field midway to the village we can cut for hay early. Would a clear space this afternoon give your crew time to set up their booths for a fair day tomorrow?"

"It would," Saint said. "It would indeed."

FIFTEEN

The field was mowed, fresh hay piled high to dry at the edges, before the day was out, and the crew of *Vainglorious Rose* were busy at setting up their booths well into the evening. Some of those in the village had made booths of their own to sell their crafts and foodstuffs at regular market days, and so joined the visitors in the field. Both groups seemed to welcome the other's presence and a bit of early trading and gaming went on well into the night.

Denholm invited Captain Saint and his officers to dine in the farmhouse with him and Lynelle. Saint accepted, bringing his first mate and a young man of perhaps twenty who he introduced as his nephew.

"Thank you, Mistress Carew," Saint said as Lynelle cleared the plates after they'd eaten. "Many thanks. As fine a plate as I've had before me since we left Eidera, no question."

"Just a bit of chicken and potatoes, Captain Saint," she said. "Simple fare."

"We're simple men, we spacers, Mistress Carew," Saint's first mate, Crandall, said. "After weeks of beef grown in the *Rose's* nutrient vats, a bit of home cooking sits quite right by us."

"Well, thank you for your kind words, Mister Crandall." She nodded. "Captain Saint's, as well." She glanced at the third visitor, but the lad remained as quiet as he had throughout the meal.

"Thank your hostess, lad," Saint said, nudging the boy with his foot under the table.

"Was good," the lad muttered sullenly. "Thank'ee."

Saint scowled. "My sister's boy," he said to Denholm. "A surly lad, but he does his work." He reached into a bag beside his chair and pulled out a bottle. "If you've no objection here, I've a bit of spirits from Eidera?"

"No objection from us," Denholm said. "My hands make a drink from the potatoes, but it's harsh stuff. We haven't had the time or resources to age a proper spirit."

Saint laughed. "I wouldn't call this proper, myself." He drained his glass of water and poured from the bottle, then did the same for the others. "It's a corn whiskey, and young, but it does the job."

"Is it a profitable trade, Captain Saint?" Lynelle asked, returning to the table and her own drink. "These small cargoes and amusements?"

"Enough for me and my crew to live and put a bit by. It's a free life we lead, though, and that's what we want more than wealth. We —"

He was interrupted by a loud, trumpeting sound from his nephew's seat. The boy laughed loudly, exposing a mouthful of teeth in a condition almost as distressing as the sound and smell emanating from his place.

"Horsfall!" Saint said. "Take yourself to the privy, lad!"

"It's up the stairs between the bedrooms," Lynelle said, wincing.

Saint waited until Horsfall had left the room, then sighed.

"My apologies, Mistress Carew. The lad was far from civilized when he came aboard and I'm afraid my crew has done little to tumble off the edges."

"Of course, Captain Saint." She gave a rueful smile and glanced at Denholm. "It's not the worst thing to be brought to my table."

Denholm grimaced. "Boots straight from the pigs *one* time, and it's never forgotten."

Saint laughed and his first mate joined in.

———

THE FAIR DAY itself went well.

While the crew of *Vainglorious Rose* and their entertainments were certainly weighted to separate fair-goers from whatever coin they might have in the most efficient way possible, Denholm saw nothing to indicate it might be more so than his indentures, a somewhat experienced group themselves in such things, might expect. In fact, a table in the gaming tent seemed to have been set aside for those who wished to place more on side bets on which player could most effectively cheat the others than in the pot itself.

One of the *Vainglorious Roses* was a woodcarver of no little skill, and Denholm put him in touch with the youngsters of the village with an entrepreneurial bent, who then spent the day scavenging for knots, burls, and branches of *varrenwood* which would otherwise have become scrap.

"I could've negotiated better terms, Mister Carew," Denholm's foreman said, "and got the coin direct to the holding."

"It's a pittance, Harting," Denholm said. He smiled as two girls hauled a heavy burl up to the woodcarver's bench and began haggling. The wood would be lovely when carved and polished, but the piece was too small to be made into the veneers it would be profitable to ship back to the Core. "It keeps the children out of trouble in the other tents and gives them a taste of commerce." He grinned widely as the two girls picked up the burl and began walking away, only to be called back by the woodcarver with a better offer and the addition of some carved toys. "I expect we'll see consortiums forming before the day's out. In fact, there may be a small market to other artists in those bits, and it wouldn't hurt for the holding's children to manage it."

"There's weeding and picking in the fields for the little buggers to earn their keep," Harting muttered. "Not picking through what's not theirs to start with."

"We don't indenture children on my lands, Harting," Denholm said, letting his tone grow a little harsh. "I've told you that before and I'll not have them set to work for the holding, no matter what you're used to."

"You're young, yourself, Mister Carew, perhaps the experience of others would —"

"I've given them my permission to sell the scrap, Harting, and that's the end of it. Leave them be."

"As you say, sir."

Harting tugged his forelock and scuttled away. It was a gesture the man had grown up with on his home planet, an archaic gesture of submission those settlers had brought back, and it irritated Denholm to no end — not so much due to the subservience it implied, but because he suspected Harting's use of it held more insolence than anything else.

"Tha' mon was a poor choice o' foreman, love."

Denholm turned and took the plate of fried dough covered in sugar Lynelle held out to him. He took a bite before responding, not minding that it was still so hot from the fryer that it burned his mouth and he had to suck air around the mouthful to cool it. He thought that Captain Saint and *Vainglorious Rose* might be onto something with their traveling fair, as having their own ship allowed them to carry luxuries a colony wouldn't necessarily order for themselves. Sweets especially, as sugar was still dear and in short supply on Dalthus. There was cane sugar shipped up from holdings in the south and he and Mylin both planned to have a field or two of sugar beets for the next season, but the processing was a major investment when most of the colony was only just able to put enough fresh calories on every plate.

Moreover, with so little produced on-planet as yet, the indentures had little to spend their wages on locally, so had plenty to spare for the *Vainglorious Rose's* wares.

"The best of the lot, unfortunately," Denholm said, returning to Lynelle's comment.

"Oh, I ken, I do." Lynelle took a bite of her own treat. "Old enow to command a bit o' respect and offset our youth."

"And not transported for some crime or with so much debt as to show he's irresponsible, as so many of those after the first arrivals have been." He sighed. "We'll keep an eye out and replace him when we can. Until then —"

"It's make do," Lynelle nodded. "Aye."

SIXTEEN

"So it's settled then?" Denholm asked.

He had the images of six other settlers on his tablet, Sewall Mylin one of them, as well as the latest transport schedule for colony's lone antigrav hauler. The five other than he and Mylin also had large tracts of *varrenwood* and the group was discussing the use of the Carew-Mylin mill for cutting their raw lumber before export.

They'd built the mill with capacity to spare, anticipating the growth of *varrenwood* exports from his and the Mylins' lands. Mylin's contribution of one of his own motors to complement Denholm's made the mill even more efficient, and there was no way that their own hands could keep it supplied with raw lumber at this early stage. None of the others had been able to put up a mill with similar capabilities, and the addition of two of Mylin's sons running wagons from the mill to Landing with the finished product made it an even better opportunity for the others to have their raw logs milled there.

They could make use of the antigrav hauler to move their logs directly from the logging site to Denholm's mill, then the wagons saved them the cost of having the hauler bring them to Landing for storage. Since the logs weren't perishable, they were also able to fit into the hauler's regular schedule as space was available and save on those transport costs.

"I believe so," one of the other men said, "so long as there's a bit of flexibility in the schedule of wh —"

His image stuttered, then froze, bright blocks of pixelization covering it. At the same time a status indicator at the top of the tablet began flashing. Denholm frowned and tapped it, as he could see others doing before several of their images also froze. His frown deepened as he saw that the alert was that one of the satellites in the constellation had dropped offline. The others would reroute the video feed in a moment, but it was unusual for the hearty, heavily protected satellites they'd brought with them to fail.

The number of failed satellites quickly changed to two, then three.

"What in the hell's going on —"

"Was there debris we mis —"

The settlers still in the conference were talking over each other in surprise.

Another alert drew Denholm's attention, this one deemed less important than the failed satellites by his tablet. A ship had transitioned from *darkspace* at the Dalthus IV lunar L_1 point — the Lagrangian point midway between the planet and its moon — at nearly the same time as the first failure, only seconds before. A fourth satellite failed and the system finally noted that all of those which had failed were those which could scan the local space around Dalthus. The satellites which were strictly for communications or positioning on the planet itself were all intact.

Denholm's blood chilled and he leaned toward his tablet, keying it to send those alerts to everyone in the conference.

"Gentlemen! I believe we are under some sort of attack."

DENHOLM'S TABLET screen was more crowded with images than before. Most of the colonists were viewing this discussion, some six days after the ship had first arrived and attacked their satellites, but only the most vocal two dozen or so were represented on screen. The majority were content to watch and listen — and form sides in the ongoing debate about what to do.

"The Brogdons and Tooleys, now the Pennings," Heallstede Kinder said. "I say give them what they've asked for and send them on their way."

The attacking ship — pirates, Denholm allowed, though it shook him to admit they were really having to deal with pirates — had destroyed all of the satellites capable of telling the colonists what was happening in space around the planet, leaving them only with communications and location capabilities, and those rather limited. Then had come the first attack on a settlement.

The Brogdons were a mid-sized holder, with perhaps a dozen indentures. The attackers left one alive to confirm what had happened, the twelve-year old son of an indenture.

The message the pirates broadcast after was simple and direct. Video of the attack and destruction, followed by a shadowy figure and a distorted voice.

Give us what we want in a lump sum, or we'll take it piecemeal.

The destruction of the Tooley holding confirmed what piecemeal would look like.

"It's not so much they want, when it's all of us providing it," Kinder went on. "It's wool, not mutton, these men are after. We'll be able to survive and rebuild with what we have left."

He looked down at his tablet as it *pinged*, indicating that someone else wanted to respond to him. Kinder winced, but tapped his screen.

"Get your head out of your sheep, Heallstede," Lillee Bocook shouted, "and remember the shearer comes back a second time and more! Give in now and we'll see them again for more once we've rebuilt!"

Denholm winced as well at her tone. Bocook was a strong woman, and Denholm respected her, but she seemed to have no middle in her. A man was either a genius or a fool to Lillee Bocook, and which usually depended on whether he agreed with her in any given moment.

"She's the right of it," Lynelle said quietly from the other side of the kitchen table.

"She does." Denholm shook his head. "But he won't take kindly to her tone."

"Better sheared than dead!" Kinder was yelling back.

"I say we fight!" Bocook yelled.

"There's too bloody many of them, you daft woman! And anywhere on the planet they can strike next! How're we to even know where to —"

Denholm sighed with relief as the moderator of the discussion muted both Bocook and Kinder. He could see both their points. On the one hand it galled him to give in and pay what the pirates demanded. The sum was large, and it would take the whole colony to assemble that much in coin or equivalent goods, but it wouldn't break them — not the larger holders, at least. On the other hand, even if they could bring together enough of a force, there was no way to know where to strike at the pirates. The bastards could sit up there in their ship and attack at will anywhere on the planet, while the settlers had only a single craft capable of flight.

"I'll have no truck with name-calling and fighting amongst ourselves," Wickam Doakes said into the silence. As he'd used his share in the colony to purchase a lease on the chandlery concession and appointment as Crown agent, he was moderating the discussion. "It's one thing for you lot to go on and on when we're in conclave at Landing, but not like this. Not now. I say Mister Kinder's said his piece and we'll move on ... Mister Coalson's next in the queue, so speak your piece, Mister Coalson."

"Och, but he'll hae a fix fer things, sure," Lynelle muttered.

Denholm nodded absently, eyes fixed on his tablet as Coalson spoke.

"While I tend to agree with Mistress Bocook that these men will likely return for more if we pay them, Mister Kinder does have the right of it that we're in no position to fight, either. We haven't the slightest idea where they'll land next and we certainly can't attack their ship in orbit." Coalson shrugged. "I think, perhaps, we must consider a third option, distasteful as it may be — do nothing and wait them out."

There was a flurry of pings as others in the conference demanded attention. Coalson waited, then nodded.

"Yes, I'm certain you all dislike the option as much as I do, but what choice do we really have? Beggar ourselves paying tribute and then wait to be fleeced again? Assemble some force and hope to catch these men by sheer luck, all the while leaving our own holdings undefended?"

Denholm sighed and tapped his screen to indicate he had something to say in response. He'd honestly hoped things between him and Rashae Coalson would come to an end after that ridiculous duel, or, at least, after they'd each gone off to their own holdings with thousands of kilometers between them, but Coalson's positions were so opposed to his own that Denholm found himself unable to not speak up.

He expected Coalson to ignore him and choose someone else to speak, but to his surprise the man selected him.

"Yes, Carew, you have something to say?"

"Only that I'm wondering," Denholm said, "how it is we're to sit and do nothing while our neighbors are slaughtered and their holdings looted and burned. Seems a hard, cold thing."

"Indeed," Coalson said, "but that's not at all what I'm suggesting, and I'm shocked you'd think it of me."

"What are you suggesting, then, if we're not to fight or pay these men?"

"I suggest, Carew, that we examine their targets and learn from them. The Brogdon, Tooley, and Penning holdings are all of a type. Mid-sized holdings, and isolated — they had, what, a dozen or two dozen indentures each? Not nearly enough to fight off an attack, and therefore vulnerable."

Denholm frowned. Coalson sounded calm and reasonable, which was so unlike the man that it made Denholm suspicious.

"Wha's tha mon up to?" Lynelle asked, echoing Denholm's thoughts.

"I've studied what imagery and sensor readings we have of this ship," Coalson went on, "and concluded that there can be no more than one hundred or, perhaps, one hundred fifty men aboard. Some of those must be left behind to man the ship during their raids, and they'll obviously want to significantly outnumber their targets, being the cowards that they are. Landing and the other free towns are certainly safe from them, as are the larger holdings, and most of the very small holders are located near each other in their little bands and villages. They've barely enough in the way of portable wealth and goods to make it worth the pirates' while in any case."

Denholm glanced over at Lynelle to see her reaction, but her attention was focused on her tablet — brow furrowed and tapping rapidly. She'd always been irritated by Coalson's easy dismissal of those settlers who'd had only enough colony shares for a bit of land. In his view, anyone who'd come to Dalthus simply to build a small home for themselves was a fool and should have stayed behind.

"No," Coalson said, "it's the mid-sized holdings, where there's some wealth to plunder and fewer holders and indentures for them to fight, there's where they'll strike." He shook his head and frowned. "Sadly, as Mister Kinder pointed out for us, we've still no way of knowing which exactly they'll strike, so confronting them is out of the question."

"So what is it you suggest, Mister Coalson?" Doakes asked.

Coalson shrugged. "I'd think it was obvious. We must remove these marauders' targets until they seek prey and profit elsewhere.

The mid-size holders, those at most risk from these attacks, should seek shelter at the larger holdings until the danger has passed."

There was a new flurry of *pings* as others sought to be recognized and speak. Coalson chose one.

"And what's to happen with our goods and livestock!" Bailie Arthur demanded.

"Well, you'd certainly have to leave most of that behind on your holdings," Coalson said, his tone mild. "With just the one hauler we couldn't move *everything*, after all."

"So your *suggestion* is we leave all we have to these bastards for the taking? And then have nothing when they leave?"

"You'll have your lives," Coalson said, "and I'm told some feel that's a great deal." He shrugged. "And your lands, of course. These pirates can't take the very land with them. I'm certain something could be worked out to assist you in rebuilding after they've left."

Arthur's jaw clenched. "At a price, no doubt."

"Well —"

"That's you to a T, Coalson! Ever after a bit of what someone else calls their own!"

"And what should I do, then?" Coalson asked, his temper showing now. "Who'll bear the brunt of the tribute this pirate demands? We larger holders, that's who — for we'll hear nothing but whingeing about how little it leaves you if we demand others pay a fair share. If they take your stock and burn your holding, I'm to give you shelter and make you whole for nothing in return? Why exactly?"

"Some common bloody humanity!"

"No, Mister Arthur, you chose to come to Dalthus without a means to protect what's yours, it's not on me or mine to do it for you. I offer you and your kind a safe place to ride this out and —"

"My 'kind', is it? Why you insufferable, self —"

"Gentlemen!" Doakes broke in, cutting both men off. "This argument does neither of you any credit." There was a muted *ping* as someone sought his attention. "Yes, perhaps a more reasonable voice

—" He looked down at his tablet. "— or ... well ..." Doakes sighed. "Yes, Mistress Carew?"

Denholm looked across the table in surprise as Lynelle began speaking into her tablet.

"Much as it pains me tae say so aboot such a mon, it may be that Mister Coalson has stumbled all a'blind into tha right of it."

Denholm blinked.

"Well, nae the schemin', selfish, graspin' fer profit in another man's misery-pile part, ya ken, but tha bit aboot where they'll strike, perhaps."

"Lynelle!"

"Miss Carew — really!"

"If you ken where they've struck," Lynelle went on, ignoring Denholm's and Doakes' protests, "you can see that Mister Coalson has stumbled close to it. But there's the how, then, isn't there? How'd they ken where ta strike? Which holdings tha' have some wealth, but nae so many hands as to make a fight of it?"

Lynelle tapped her tablet and a list holdings appeared on his. Denholm studied it, as he was certain the other holders would be, but didn't understand. True, the Brogdon, Tooley, and Penning holdings were on it, but in the third, seventh, and eleventh positions. The intervening spaces were filled with both larger holdings and groups of smaller holders who'd formed close associations. The Carew's own holding topped the list.

Denholm glanced across the table.

"What —"

"The holders who had a bit of a fair day last month," Lynelle said. "That bloody Saint and his fuzzy-toothed nephew scouting aboot and seein' who had what goods and how many hands." She scowled. "They made a bloody list, an' now they're back and working their way down it."

Denholm looked back to the list. Brogdon, Tooley, and Penning — in order, if one skipped over those holdings and groups too large for a single ship's crew to attack. In order, which meant ...

"Aye," Lynelle said, highlighting the next mid-size holding on the list. "And if we know who's next —" She gave a nod toward Bailie Arthur's image on her tablet. His holding was just after the Pennings on the list, with only a single large holding between them. "— we can set the buggers a stalking horse."

SEVENTEEN

The air inside the barn on the Arthurs' holding was hot and dense with the scent of animals and the men packed inside.

Denholm closed his eyes and rested his forehead against the rough-hewn wood of the wall. At least there was a bit of fresh, predawn breeze coming through a gap in the boards next to him. After a full day and night packed into the barn, waiting for the expected attack, he was heartily sick of it and ready for a change.

Lynelle's realization that the pirates were, in fact, the same men as the traveling fair and had used those fairs as a way to scout the Dalthus holdings for likely targets had altered the course of the debate. Even Rashae Coalson, once he'd seen the inevitable result of the vote, Denholm assumed, had joined in the consensus to establish a force at the Arthurs' holding and fight.

Coalson and his men were even now packed tightly in the Arthurs' indenture barracks along with volunteers from several other holdings, much as Denholm was packed into the barn. Others, all hurriedly flown to the Arthurs' by the colony's lone antigrav hauler under cover of darkness, were in the farmhouse itself and the other outbuildings.

Altogether, they'd assembled a force of over two hundred from around the planet. Some, like Denholm, were armed with modern laser rifles they'd brought from the Core, but most held more primitive chemical propellant arms, some hurriedly printed by the limited manufactury in Landing.

The pirates, if the assumption of a single ship was correct, would have less men than that, though would be better armed. The sites of the three other attacks had shown damage from mostly laser weapons and the occasional flechette.

A trickle of dust and hay fell from above and Denholm stifled a sneeze. He also stifled his concerns for Lynelle who was in the hayloft above him armed with another laser rifle. She'd refused to stay behind, insisting that, "If the clan's to battle go, I'll nae be left behind."

He had to admit she was the better shot, and sniping from the hayloft should keep her safe, but he was worried nonetheless.

Early the day before, in the back of the hauler on the way here, she'd been pale and short of breath. She claimed it was from the close-packed quarters of the hauler and its motion, but the inertial compensators made a hauler's motion barely detectable. Then they arrived and she rushed from the hauler's ramp to lean one hand on a landing strut and vomit. Denholm rushed to her side, but she waved his concerns off and grasped her rifle, rushing to the barn to get under cover as quickly as possible.

After that there'd been little time to speak as they'd settled into the crowded barn to wait.

Denholm opened his eyes. The Arthurs and their hands were stirring outside, leaving the house and barracks in a semblance of their normal morning routines. That each of them had a sidearm concealed on their person and that there were more rifles concealed about the holding wasn't visible to the casual observer. They might be in for another long, hot day of waiting — the pirates had struck other holdings in the dead of night when everyone was sleeping. They might hold to that, or they might change that routine, if they suspected holdings would now be more watchful in the dark.

Or we could be entirely wrong about where they'll strike next.

That was what Denholm feared now more than the possibility of a fight here.

If the pirates struck elsewhere, the consensus to fight which had brought this force together might dissolve back into squabbling over whether to appease them or not.

Denholm frowned and that concern disappeared as he noted a growing rumble. The sun was just enough over the horizon to make looking in its direction blinding, and that was the direction the pirates chose to attack from. The rumble grew to a roar and those outside the shelter of buildings ran for prearranged positions. The pirates' boat slammed heavily to the ground in the farmyard and its ramps dropped, giving Denholm his first look at the enemy.

The boat looked familiar, though he couldn't swear it was the same. Some of the men rushing down the ramps wore armor. Mismatched sets and pieces, he was relieved to see, with not a complete set anywhere, and none of it powered — if the pirates had modern combat armor, then things would go badly for the settlers.

The pirates began firing even as they rushed from their boat, striking down those exposed workers who'd hesitated or had too far to run to a place of shelter. Denholm ground his teeth at the need to hold fire as those men were hit, but if they opened fire while the pirates were close enough to retreat onto their boat, then the whole plan would be for naught. They had just this one chance to end it — if the pirates escaped here they'd have no way of telling where the next attack would come.

The attackers spread out from the boat, firing indiscriminately as they went. Denholm readied his rifle — they were almost far enough from the boat now, moving toward the barracks and farmhouse, which put the barn and Denholm's men on their flank.

A shot rang out from the barracks.

Too soon, Denholm thought, even as he opened fire as well now that the attackers were alerted.

More shots, interspersed with the sharper *crack* of the few lasers.

The pirates hesitated, some fell as they were hit, others jerked and ducked. Then there were shouts and the attackers began falling back toward their boat.

Denholm fired again, ignoring the shouts and cheers around him in the barn. The men might think they were winning, but Denholm knew they, all of Dalthus, were in serious trouble if the pirates managed to reach their boat and take off. It wasn't enough to drive them away from this one holding, they had to destroy their ability to attack again.

"Target the boat!" he yelled.

His stomach fell as he realized it wouldn't be enough. His own shots, aimed at what he thought might be the boat's more vulnerable areas, seemed to have no effect on the craft's tough hull. The pirates took shelter amongst the boat's landing struts and behind its ramps to give covering fire as their brethren reboarded.

Bailie Arthur, firing from his farmhouse along with his family and workers, must have realized it as well. Realized that if the pirates managed to lift off his own holding might be safe, but others would be destroyed in retaliation. And the farmhouse was closest to the boat.

Denholm watched in horror as Arthur, his eldest son and daughter, and three of their hands poured from the house's door and shattered windows to rush the pirates' boat.

The pirates shifted their fire and the Arthurs were cut down before they'd even reached the boat's shadow.

The last of the pirates rushed up the boat's ramps and Denholm prepared to rush from the barn himself. Perhaps, once all the pirates were aboard and unable to fire, they might be able to get close enough to damage the boat. Or perhaps firing from underneath before it rose too far, they might strike some vulnerable site.

The rumble of the boat's engines deepened and its ramps started to close. It began to rise off the ground. Denholm drew breath to shout encouragement to those around him, call for them to follow, when he heard a new, deeper rumble. It grew louder and the colony's hauler dropped out of the sky toward the pirate boat.

The hauler, twice the size of the boat, settled over it, moving with it as the pirate's pilot tried to reach a clear space to rise.

Denholm was sick at the risk the hauler's pilot was taking with so valuable a resource. That hauler was the colony's only transport. It would be years before they accumulated enough wealth from exports to purchase another. The pilot, Witcomb Hatridge, was risking his family's future as well. He'd put his shares into the purchase of that hauler and a ninety-nine year lease on the transport concession. Even if it wasn't destroyed, being out of service for too long would ruin him.

The pirate boat rose until it was so near Denholm thought it touched the hauler, the pirates playing chicken and trying to force Hatridge to avoid them. But Hatridge was having none of it. He played the massive craft as he had daily around the colony, piloting it into tiny forest clearings or through narrow clefts to reach mining sites.

He matched the boat's rise, then reversed, settling the massive hauler gently but firmly against the boat's hull and trusting its heavy construction against the lighter craft. He settled it further, tilting as both craft lowered, the boat's engines winding up to a high pitched whine as they struggled to push against more mass than they'd ever been meant to lift.

The pirate boat struck first, its tail and engines swung through the farmhouse's second floor and then part of the first, sending debris in a wide arc. The starboard landing struts struck the ground at an angle and snapped, which sent the side of the craft plowing into the turf beyond.

Hatridge righted the hauler, skimming its starboard side inches away from the ground and slamming the port against the top of the boat. That drove the boat firmly to the ground. Its port landing struts held, digging deep furrows as the boat came to a stop listing heavily to one side.

The hauler rose quickly, moving off to a distance beyond the effective range of the pirates' weapons.

Denholm clenched his jaw. He knew it wasn't over — even with their boat disabled, the pirates wouldn't just give up. They knew what was in store for them if they surrendered and would fight to avoid it.

Even as he thought that, he could see the boat's ramps opening further and figures moving about. Shots and lasers crossed the space between the holding's buildings and the boat, but Denholm thought they might have arrived at an impasse. The range and cover each side held made targeting difficult. The air around him was rich with scents of the wood walls, raw where projectiles shot it through and burned where lasers struck.

There was movement at one of the boat's ramps and he thought for a moment that the pirates would attempt to rush the holding's buildings.

Then from within the shadows the crystalline tube of a ship's gun probed forward.

Denholm had a bare moment's terror — for himself, the men around him, and for Lynelle firing from the hayloft above — before the world dissolved into flame-lit darkness, smoke, and screams.

EIGHTEEN

"Lynelle!"

The holding after the battle seemed unnaturally quiet despite the shouts of men and women rushing about. Cries of joy or despair rose as the fate of loved ones and friends was discovered.

Denholm lifted another of the barn's burned and shattered boards and tossed it aside. There were pockets of heat where the rubble smoldered. Luckily nothing had been set afire outright.

"Lynelle!"

In the long minutes after the pirates' cannon fired, Denholm hadn't had time to think of anything beyond the moment.

The ship's cannon, designed to punch through a tough thermoplastic hull in the vacuum of *darkspace* behaved much differently in atmosphere and against the wooden walls of a building. It struck over a wider area and explosively boiled what moisture was left in the wood, causing the side of the structure to explode in charred cinders.

Some men inside were killed outright, others fell, bleeding from splinters or burns, while the rest crouched behind what cover remained.

With the shelter of the boat and a heavy weapon, the pirates would obliterate the holding if the settlers stayed in place. Despite the risk, they had to attack.

Denholm had little recollection of the battle. He remembered picking himself up, shrugging off splinters and boards, and yelling something that caused others to follow. Those in the farmhouse and barracks must have had the same thought, for men and women poured out of those as well.

The pirates managed to fire the gun once more, destroying what was left of the farmhouse, before the holders overran them. Once the boat's ramps were secure and the remaining pirates had been taken prisoner, Denholm rushed back to the barn, which had collapsed further.

Now he had time to think — time to worry, as he'd not seen Lynelle once in the fighting.

"*Lynelle!*"

He tossed another board aside, looking for anything that would tell him where the hayloft had been.

"Is it thinking I've nae the wits to leave a burning building you're about, love?"

Denholm spun around. She was there — singed, sooty, and resting her weight on her rifle, but whole and safe. He rushed to her and engulfed her in his arms, noting that she was squeezing him back just as hard.

"I thought —"

"Nae more than I did, seeing you rush toward their guns, you daft —"

He shut her mouth with a kiss, only stopping when someone loudly cleared his throat nearby.

"Mister Carew, sir, could we see you t'other side o' the boat, sir?"

Denholm took a step back, wiping his eyes. He looked to the man who'd spoken.

"What? Why?"

"One o' the pirates we took, sir, he's asking if you're here and to see you."

Denholm frowned. Why would the pirate — likely Saint, as that was the only one he'd really spoken to — want to see him specifically?

He closed his eyes again and grasped Lynelle, inhaling her scent through the smoke and soot, then stepped back.

"All right, lead on, then."

Denholm crossed the farmyard to where the surviving pirates had been lined up. Several were prone, their injuries being tended by their fellows, though given their almost certain fate he wondered at the logic of that. Others knelt, hands lashed behind them. One stood, blood streaking his face from a blow to the head and soaking his pant leg where he'd been shot.

Saint spat to the side. "Carew, eh?"

"Captain Saint."

"Well." The pirate looked around at the destruction and grunted. "What were it? That brought you here, I mean."

"You went in order," Denholm said. "Of the holdings you visited for your 'fairs'." He nodded toward Lynelle who had moved to the side and held her rifle not-quite pointed at Saint. "It was Lynelle that saw the pattern."

Saint grunted again, but nodded to Lynelle. "Mistress Carew." He shrugged when Lynelle said nothing. "Never thought of that — what with skippin' the larger ones and all." He sighed. "What's it for us, then?"

Denholm looked around at the bodies being lined up for burial and the injured being treated before transport back to their holdings. The shouts of those looking for missing friends had died down, replaced by angry murmurs as the full butcher's bill became known. Near the farmhouse the remaining Arthurs, Bailie's wife, Catherine, and two children, were hunched over the still bodies.

"Much as you'd expect, I suppose, captain."

"Yes, as to that ..." He wiped at the blood on his face and winced, then probed his scalp as fresh blood flowed. "May be as there's a bit of negotiationing to be done yet."

"I doubt that," Denholm said. "I imagine the pleasure of seeing your neck stretched will far outweigh anything you have to offer."

"Oh, don't go misbelieving me, Mister Carew." Saint shifted his weight and winced. "I don't suppose you'd care to sit and discuss it?" He shrugged as Denholm shook his head. "Very well, then. I asked for you specific-like, for you seemed an honest, decent sort — you and your missus. Treated us well, hosted us to dinner and such." He spat again. "More than could be said for most."

"Hospitality I regret, I assure you."

"As may be, but you seem a decent sort, as I said. Not the sort to take treacherousness at all lightly — and there's treacherousness more than mine about this world, Mister Carew. Such as a man like you'd have no truck with. You've no idea who you've —" He broke off and glanced past Denholm. "You —"

Denholm jerked to the side, startled by the *crack* of ionizing air seemingly right next to him. Saint's right eye disappeared and he dropped to the ground.

Denholm looked first toward Lynelle, thinking it was her who'd shot, but the shot had been on his other side and Lynelle was looking that way as well, rifle half raised to her shoulder.

He looked that way in time to see Rashae Coalson lower his laser rifle and stalk forward, a dozen of his men at his back.

"What —"

"Pirate scum," Coalson muttered, walking up to Saint's body and kicking it.

NINETEEN

The remaining pirates were taken to Landing. The trial, such as it was, was short and to the point. Presided over by Wickam Doakes, in his role as Crown agent, the closest thing to a magistrate Dalthus would see for some time. A few of the pirates maintained that they'd been aboard the boat the entire time and had no hand in the attacks themselves, hadn't even known Saint's intentions when they'd come aboard his ship, but the verdicts remained the same for all.

They were hung on hastily erected gibbets along the edge of the landing field. Rashae Coalson and some few others argued for the bodies to be tarred and left to rot in place as a warning to others, but Denholm and most of the other colonists balked at that. Instead, the bodies were taken down and buried immediately.

Denholm watched sadly as the last of the pirates was cut down. One of these was the woodcarver who'd bought his *varrenwood* scraps. He wondered what had brought a man with such talent to choose piracy instead ... and what he might say to the children back on the holding who'd sold the man wood and delighted in the toys he'd carved in return.

He felt a comforting hand on his shoulder and slid his arm around Lynelle.

The crowd began to disperse, filing off the landing field onto the one thoroughfare in Landing that could be called a street and not a cartpath. The town was growing, double in size from what it had been just after planetfall and the dispersion of settlers to their hold-ings, but it was still small. Past the standing buildings on that first street though, the beginnings of a plan had been laid out. Within another year the population and size would likely double again. There was talk of cobbling the main street, at least until the colony had the means of producing proper paving.

Stakes and rope marked lots that would be sold to those looking to make a start there — either released indentures or colonists who'd sold their lands after a bad start and chose to try their hand at merchant- or craft-life in town. The crowd moved toward one of those lots now.

It was designated as a public park in the town's plan, but was a simple square of unmown field now. Paths were worn through the tough, native ground cover, showing where people's travels naturally took them.

A tall pillar had been erected at the lot's center. One hundred forty-six names were carved into the pillar's base — all of those who died on the three obliterated holdings and in the battle at the Arthurs'. It had been printed and erected in the midst of the trial and the ceremony to dedicate it scheduled for immediately after the last pirate hanged. If there'd been a bit of doubt about the pirates' guilt, Denholm might have questioned the fairness of that.

Bryson Malcomson led off the ceremony with an ancient tune played on bagpipes. The haunting sound floated over the silent crowd — most had their heads bowed, others stared at the pillar in silence.

"Hmph."

Lynelle was staring at Malcomson with narrowed eyes.

"What?" Denholm asked. "I'd have thought you'd be happy to

hear those played here. It's a long time since you've been home to New Edinburgh and we likely won't ever visit there again."

"Happy? By a bloody *Malcomson?*"

Denholm suppressed a smile that wouldn't be appropriate for the occasion. He'd long ago given up understanding the long and complex list of feuds and familial dislikes Lynelle kept in her head.

"Besides which," Lynelle went on, "the pipes are nae for mourning, love. They're for the battle." She scowled at the player. "No *true* New Edinburghan would play them such." She turned her scowl skyward. "Though I can hope the sound reaches those bastards left, wherever they may be, an' chills their very dreams."

Some days after the battle at the Arthurs' holding, a merchantman arrived in-system and reported the space around Dalthus was empty of other ships. Where the remaining pirates had sailed for, they didn't know.

Lynelle's scowl deepened. "Especially that fuzzy-toothed shite, Saint's nephew."

"He's but a lad, Lynelle, perhaps this setback will set him, and the rest of them, on a different track."

Lynelle patted his arm.

"You've a good heart, love, and a forgiving nature, but blood runs true, it does." She sighed and rested a hand on her belly. Denholm watched that with concern. She'd been ill a number of times in the days since the battle with the pirates, but waved off his suggestions she see the doctor while they were already in Landing. "I suppose that means our son will be as forgiving and not ken a proper feud."

"I'm sure you'll manage to teach him the workings of ..." Denholm's eyes widened. "Wait ... what?"

TWENTY

"Pig! Here, pig! Come on, then!"

A gust of heavy wind from the storm struck him and Denholm slipped, going to his knees in the cold mud of the pen, made colder and wetter by the driving rains. This was one of the heavier storms they'd found crossed the plains of Dalthus once or twice a year, springing up with little warning and sometimes covering an area for days at a time, and he wanted all of the livestock inside the protection of the original domed barn. That would hold up to even one of the larger tornadoes sometimes spawned by these storms, better, at least, than the other outbuildings made from native materials would.

He got to his feet, arms spread wide, and approached the pig, a large sow and stubborn. All of the others had been quick enough to follow the fenced corridor he'd put up to lead them toward the barn, but this one didn't want to leave the pen, even with the storm and rain.

Lightning flashed brightly and the sow squealed, then dashed toward him. He tried to get out of the way, but his leg, already aching from the storm, betrayed him. The sow's shoulder clipped his leg and he went down again, this time face first and full length into the muck-and-worse that filled the pen.

He rose to hands and knees, spitting what had got in his mouth, but unable to even wipe his face because all the rest of him was just as covered with the filth.

"You're bacon, damn your eyes!" He got to his feet and raised his face to the rain, letting that wash some of it away, at least. "Bacon and hams, come harvest time, you! Mark my words!"

Eyes cleared of the muck, at least, he looked around the pen. The sow was halfway down the fenced path, snuffling at the edge of the barn door.

"Bloody pigs."

He made his way after her, pulling the pen's gate closed so that she couldn't return to it. The sow seemed to have decided she'd had enough of the storm, though, and waited patiently for him to slide the barn's door open just enough for her to enter and join the others.

Denholm followed, latched the door firmly, and clambered out of the fenced off area for the pigs. The rest of the barn was divided for the other animals. Horses, cows, the various fowl that made up the farm, all crowded into very little space. What had been enough to hold all their livestock when they'd first arrived, with room left over for equipment and workspaces, was now barely enough to shelter the critical animals alone. There were still more of the pigs and cows in the native-built barns — more vulnerable, but at least the best of the breeding stock was safe here.

"Lynelle!" Denholm called.

She'd been getting the last of the horses in, despite Denholm's protestations that one of the hands could help him with that and she shouldn't be out in the storm in her condition. That had earned him a look, and, truthfully, she'd been right that the farmhands were better put to use down in the village helping the folk there prepare for the storm. What they were experiencing now was only the very edges and it would only get worse for the next several hours.

"Lynelle! Pigs're all in!" he called again.

There was no answer and he wondered if she'd gone back to the house already, but that didn't seem like her and he began to worry. He'd been doing that a lot as her pregnancy progressed. Worrying that all was well, worrying that she was doing too much. Worrying most recently that with the rain and wind combined with Lynelle's ... well, size, that she'd fall and hurt herself bringing in the animals.

He'd never say it to her face, of course, but he'd noticed in the last few weeks that Lynelle had developed an amusing tendency to waddle.

Denholm frowned.

The other barn doors were closed, perhaps Lynelle had gone to the house. He'd have expected her to wait for him so they could go together, but with the storm and, well, she did tend to tire more easily these days.

A dull *clang* sounded from deeper in the barn.

Denholm froze. It was only the sort of sound one would expect, a horse or cow bumping into a trough or bucket, but something about it made his blood run cold. Then it came again.

"Lynelle?"

He made his way deeper into the barn and the *clang* came again. He could tell where it was coming from now and rushed forward toward one of the horse stalls. The horse, a big, gentle carter, was wet and steaming, just brought inside and not rubbed dry.

Denholm rushed inside the stall.

Lynelle lay on the floor of the stall, eyes closed and breath coming in short, ragged gasps — one arm wrapped around her belly, the other raised toward the stall's trough to rap her knuckles on the thin metal.

He dropped to his knees beside her and clasped her hand. Her skin was cold, so cold that he could tell even with his own feeling fair to freezing from the wind and rain.

"What?"

Lynelle drew a deep breath, grimacing as though it pained her, and her voice was as ragged as her breathing was.

"Best call for Mistress Henton, love."

DENHOLM LIFTED Lynelle from the barn floor and carried her to the house, cursing all the while that he'd sent all of the hands to help prepare for the storm in the village. If he'd had even one man remain at the farmstead to help with the stock he'd have someone to send for help.

He carried Lynelle upstairs, ignoring the trail of water and mud they left behind, and stripped her wet clothes, drying her and settling her in bed before building up the fire.

The village was only a kilometer away, but he couldn't set a horse to a gallop in this storm. He'd have to go slower and it could be as much as a quarter hour before he returned. He'd tried to call someone in the village to have them bring the midwife up to the house, but no one answered — likely everyone with a tablet had left it indoors while they secured things outside in the rain and wind.

Once he was certain Lynelle was as settled as she could be, he rushed back out to the barn. He threw a bridle and saddle onto one of the riding horses and mounted.

The wind and rain seemed worse as he set off, blinding him to the path, not quite yet a road, between farmstead and village. He kept a tight grip on the reins for the horse didn't like being out in the storm and balked at every flash of lightning.

It seemed to take forever, but the lights of the village finally came into sight.

Denholm began calling out as he entered the outskirts and rode toward Mistress Henton's cottage. A tidy little place not too close to the village square, but not so far away as to make the marketing troublesome, either. He'd had to outbid three other first settlers for Henton's indenture. Doctors were hard to come by on colony worlds, most preferring the modern technologies available in the Core, so anyone with any medical knowledge, but especially around birthing, was in high demand.

A crowd of his farmhands had formed behind him as he arrived at

Henton's cottage. Denholm slid from his horse and met her at her door, struggling to make sense over the rising wind and his own breathlessness.

"Is it just the baby coming, Mister Carew?" Henton asked.

Denholm shook his head. "Something else — something's wrong."

"I'll get my bag," Henton said, then laid a hand on Denholm's forearm. "All fathers think there's something wrong when a babe comes early. It's likely just the storm brought it on and naught to worry over."

Denholm didn't care if she thought him a worrier, hoped she was correct, just so long as she came along quickly. Which she did, back in a moment with a large bag and a heavy, waterproof cloak.

He'd driven his horse hard on the ride here, harder than he should have even if the conditions were good, but some of the hands had ridden and there were other mounts available. One of the hands, Tully, a fine horseman himself, took Mistress Henton up behind him and they followed Denholm out of the village back toward the farmstead.

All the trip Denholm worried about what they'd find when they returned. That he hadn't done enough for Lynelle before he'd left for the village, or that he'd spent too much time seeing to her comfort and they'd return too late, or even that he'd put too much wood on the fire and it might have jumped the hearth and set the house ablaze.

All was much as he'd left it, though. Mistress Henton left her cloak in the mudroom and took her bag upstairs. Denholm followed.

Lynelle was lying still, her breath still ragged and it seemed shallower to Denholm. Her hair, despite how long she'd been inside, was still damp and there was a sheen of sweat on her face.

Denholm watched Henton set her bag down and check Lynelle. He waited for her to turn and smile, for her to tell him he'd worried needlessly and dragged her out into the storm for no cause.

Instead she frowned.

"May I use your tablet, Mister Carew?"

Denholm handed it over and she began tapping and swiping at it.

Every farmstead had its own data core, the technology was fairly simple and the size, even for a huge amount of information, was negligible. Learning cores for the children of the farm and village, all kinds of other information, especially that which would be needed for farming, mining, and the million other things that kept the small society going, thousands of hours of entertainment, all in one neat package. Along with a library of medical texts and instructions that everyone prayed they'd never need to access.

Henton studied the tablet. She poked and prodded at Lynelle, whispering to her and frowning at the soft responses. At one point she drew a needle from her bag and pricked Lynelle's finger, setting a drop of blood into an analyzer she plugged into Denholm's tablet. All the while frowning more and more.

She sent Denholm for a bowl of cool water and a cloth.

When he returned with it, she wet the cloth and gently bathed Lynelle's face. The two women shared a look, Henton's concerned, Lynelle's glazed, yet somehow peaceful. Denholm suspected he'd been sent for the bowl more to give them time to speak without him there than for any real need.

"Mister Carew, sir," Henton said quietly without turning. "Would you be so kind as to send to Landing for Doctor Purdue?"

TWENTY-ONE

"Aye, Denholm, I'll be ... way quick as may be."

"How long?"

Denholm gnawed the inside of his cheek with frustration. It had taken nearly a quarter hour more to raise Witcomb Hatridge and the colony's antigrav hauler. The storm blocked the signal to the satellites and it had taken that long for either the storm to weaken somewhat, though from the sounds outside that wasn't it, or for a satellite remaining after the pirate attack to draw closer.

"I'm on ... coast," Hatridge said, voice coming with odd gaps through the tablet's speaker. He paused. "Fifteen hundred kilometers ... Landing, then on to you ... two hours ... more." Another pause. "But I'll have to unload the hauler here ... it's half loaded and the inertial compensator's been ... since the pirates ... can't take the risk of the load coming loose in the storm with that not working."

"Witcomb, damn you, we need the doctor here!"

One of the farmhands laid a comforting hand on his shoulder and squeezed. Denholm didn't see who it was, the house was crowded with men and women who'd followed them back from the village. He took a deep breath, knowing he should remain calm.

"Doctor Purdue won't get ... faster if my hauler's broken up and ... across the plains from a shifting load, Denholm."

Denholm took another deep breath.

"I know, Witcomb, but ... please?"

"The lads here ... dab hands with a pallet jack ... forklift, Denholm, fast as ever ... seen. They'll have us unloaded ... quarter hour, no more, then I'm on ... way, I promise you."

"Thank you."

THE HOURS DRAGGED ON. The storm worsened, let up some, and then worsened again, while what information Denholm could get from the weather satellites showed that it had no intention of ending anytime soon.

The house, if anything, grew more crowded as men and women from the village braved the storm to visit and speak a few words, none of which Denholm could remember. Someone made a bitter herb tea, only somewhat sweetened by honey, and forced a mug into his hands. Through it all, the hauler still didn't come with the doctor and Denholm grew more and more desperate with each call he made to Hatridge, adding the doctor in Landing to the calls only increased his sense of urgency.

"Witcomb, please."

"... trying, Denholm ... swear," Hatridge's voice came from the tablet, his image and audio skipping and pausing as the storm degraded the signal. "Crew's working ... repair."

Hours ago, the crew working hurriedly to unload the hauler had damaged it. A forklift raked the craft's side, tearing open the hold and damaging an engine.

Hatridge was certain it could be repaired, but it would take time — time Denholm didn't think Lynelle had. Hatridge, though, wasn't willing to risk flying the craft at speed with that damage.

"Air gets in at speed ... rip the hold apart."

Denholm closed his eyes and nodded. He believed Hatridge would take any reasonable risk to get Doctor Purdue to Lynelle — if he said the risk was too great, then Denholm would take him at his word.

"... not wait ..." Doctor Purdue was saying. "I've two men who'll ride with me. We'll ride now and ... hauler ... along the way."

Denholm's heart fell. He should feel grateful, he supposed, that the doctor and others were willing to risk riding in the storm for hours to get to his holding, but he couldn't help but wonder how dire Lynelle's situation must be to make the doctor do so.

THE BABE CAME an hour before dawn.

Outside the storm still raged and there was no sign of Doctor Purdue nor was the hauler repaired. It seemed that every time Denholm contacted Hatridge for an update there was some new issue preventing the craft from flying.

Mistress Henton brought Denholm upstairs and left him to sit with Lynelle.

"Have y'seen our son, love? Isn't he a bonnie lad?"

Denholm squeezed Lynelle's hand. It was the third time she'd woken and asked him that and her New Edinburgh burr had grown stronger each time. Her hair was wet with sweat and her face pale and wan. Her normally brilliant green eyes were watery and unfocused, as though she were seeing something he couldn't, something a great distance away.

"I have, love," he said, as he had before. "He's a fine lad." He swallowed hard to keep his composure. "Strong, he is."

He'd been to the nearby cradle where the boy was swaddled. The lad had looked up at him, seeming to see Denholm, though he knew that wasn't possible so young. And he'd not cried yet, as though he knew that ... knew what Denholm dare not even think.

"I'm so glad it's a boy, love," Lynelle said, her eyes cleared and she stared at him with a sudden intensity. "Lord knows the proper muck you'd make o' raisin' a wee lass all on yer lonesome."

"Shh," Denholm said, smoothing the hair from her forehead. "I'll have you to set me to rights, just like always."

Lynelle shook her head. "No, love," she said. "I'm sore tore up inside and more." She winced. "E'en yer doctor gets here ... I'm done, love."

He shook his head, jaw clenched, willing her to take back what she'd said.

"Don't say that, Lynelle. It'll be but a short time — he'll see you right."

"Do you remember what I told you, love? Back on New London, a'fore we left? 'Bout bein' yer mate an' all?"

Denholm racked his memory ... back on New London? They'd been in Beal's aircar, hadn't they? On the way to the port? He'd made some joke about going for a'merchantship instead of for a colony.

Oh, God, if we only had instead. A proper surgeon aboard ... however long we wished in a modern port. Why, sweet lord, why didn't I?

He'd joked that she could be his first mate, and her eyes had flashed, "Only *mate*, by god," she'd said, "if you know what's good for you."

"I remember, love," he said, swallowing hard to hold back the tears. Hold back the despair and give her hope to keep fighting.

"Never expected this," she said. "Didn't see it coming." She grasped his hand hard. "Don't you dare live your life alone, love."

"Don't say that, Lynelle. The doctor'll be here soon."

"Don't you dare, love," she insisted. "Harlyn'll need a mother ... not just you. An' after ..."

Her brow furrowed and her gaze grew distant.

"Oh, look't what we made, love!" She smiled. "I'n't she a wonder?"

"She is," Denholm said, wanting to reassure her, but not understanding, as Harlyn was a boy.

Lynelle patted his hand.

"Y'can't see yet, love, but y'will" Lynelle said, wonder in her voice.

"Aye," Denholm said.

Lynelle grasped his hand hard, her gaze intense. "Stand by her, love. It'll be so hard fer her." Her eyes filled with tears. "So hard without a proper clan."

"I will," he said.

Lynelle's eyes cleared. She grasped his hand and stared at him. "Not only," she said. "But, by god, I'm first, y'hear me?"

"Always," he assured her.

"Bring our Harlyn over, will you, love? Then lay here and hold me? It's grown so bloody cold."

TWENTY-TWO

Denholm made his way through the crowds milling about the landing field.

The sun was strong and bright, high in the sky above Landing. The grass of the landing field was brown in late summer and dusty from lack of rain. There was a motion before the Conclave to pave the field, thinking it an improvement that would bring more merchants and shippers to the system. Denholm supposed it was a good idea, but he couldn't summon the interest to read the proposal in full. He supposed he should do that before the Conclave met the next day, but he was concerned for Harlyn, just four months old and left so many days in the care of others. More than anything he wanted to return to his home and son, but he needed more hands from the indenture ships which had arrived and wasn't comfortable giving his proxy to another holder for the Conclave vote.

He checked his tablet and looked around the crowd again, searching for the roped off section that would be his next stop. Of all the things involved in a colony world, it was these indenture fairs that Denholm still disliked the most. Unlike the first round of indentures, who were generally just those who wanted to move on and make a new life for themselves and were contracted specifically for Dalthus, many of these were men and women who'd taken to the indenture ships one step ahead of the debt collector or gaoler — or a step behind, if they were taken up and given that choice.

Three ships had arrived in-system, with over a thousand men, women, and children packed into their hulls as tightly as could be done and still make the journey around the Fringe in some semblance of health.

A fair number of holders had made their way to the port to bid on new hands, bringing with them their foremen, families, and whatever servants they felt necessary. The population of Landing was more than doubled by that, even before the crews of the three ships were counted, and the port's residents were taking full advantage of it.

Every spare bit of room, from a shared bed to folding cots, had been rented out. Every wheeled vehicle in the port was set to hire getting people to and from the landing field. And every settler or indenture with a bit of free time and any skill at craft or cooking had set themselves up with a booth of sorts at the site of the fair itself, selling all manner of food, drink, and handicrafts, or advertising more expensive wares they kept at the growing number of shops in town.

Denholm found the festive atmosphere at odds with the newly arrived indentures themselves, and in no little poor taste.

They were pale, weak, and tired from their time aboard ship. Each had a numbered, roped-off square of space on the field where they could sit and wait for a holder to come and express interest before, hopefully, making an offer. Men, women, and families who'd left their home planets for something new, and possibly better, amongst the colony worlds. Each had a story, ranging from the search for work and opportunity to being transported for debt or minor crimes, and each hoped that they'd hear a reasonable offer here on Dalthus, so as not to be herded back aboard ship for the long journey through *darkspace* to yet another world.

Denholm checked his tablet for the stall number of his next prospect then looked around to orient himself. The stall he was looking for was just across the walkway. The man was younger than Denholm would expect to have three children, still in his early twenties. He stood at the forefront of the stall, arms crossed and watching the holders wander by. His wife was at the rear of the roped off square with the children. They sat on the pile of four canvas bags which would be the only belongings the family could afford to ship with them. She had an infant in her arms and read to a younger boy from a tablet while an older girl of perhaps seven sat nearby.

The girl clutched a much-loved doll to her chest and Denholm nodded to himself. Any man who'd spend part of the tiny mass allotment indentures could afford on his child's toy was a man Denholm wanted on his lands.

"Brandon Hulse?" he asked, stepping forward and offering his hand.

"I am." The man took Denholm's hand.

"Denholm Carew. I'd speak with you if you've not yet found a place."

Hulse smiled and stepped back and spread his hands. "Step into my parlor, Mister Carew, I'd be happy to speak with you."

Denholm laughed and moved with him into the roped off space.

"Would you like to have a seat, Mister Carew?" the woman asked, starting to rise and indicating one of the canvas bags. "They're not much, but better than standing."

Denholm waved her back down. "No, thank you, Mistress Hulse. I'm comfortable on my feet and you and the children have had a long journey." He waited while she nodded thanks and settled into her place again, then said to Hulse, "You're from Waheed?"

Hulse nodded.

"Waheed's a fairly new world still — there'd be work there. Why did you leave?"

The indentures were on-planet for so little time that there was no point in not being direct in his questions. He'd read the records of each of his prospects beforehand, but some things weren't included and he wanted to hear the man's answer with his own ears. Hulse hadn't been transported for any crime, at least not officially, which put him ahead of many in this group.

Hulse scratched his neck. "My father was transported and wound up there — I'm not shamed by that, his crime wasn't mine." He paused, meeting Denholm's eye as though waiting for some reaction, then nodded as though satisfied and continued. "Mother followed him." He shrugged. "Waheed's a religious world. Not so strongly as some —" He shrugged again. "— but not mine. I don't want my children looked down on as they do there if one's not of their faith."

Denholm nodded. They talked for a time about what skills Hulse had and what he'd done on Waheed. The details were in the record and Denholm was more interested in getting a feel for the man, and the longer they spoke the more Denholm liked him.

"I've work on my home farms and a thriving lumber trade, Mister Hulse. The lumber camps are but a half-day's ride from the farm, but you'd be some days there when there's work to be done. There's a village growing quite near the farm with space for a cottage, if you've a mind, or a private room in my barracks." Denholm could see that the man was wary, waiting for the part of the offer that would make or break the deal. He considered the total he'd have to pay to hire him — the cost of transport, the commission to the indenture broker, apparently there were some small debts back on Waheed that the broker had paid and then added to the total. "Seven years — room and board in the barracks or a stipend toward that cottage I spoke of — a land grant for it at the end of your time, if you've a mind to stay on — and two shillings a fortnight."

He could tell from the look on Hulse's face that there was something amiss with the offer, but couldn't imagine what it was. At a common laborers' rate, to pay off the indenture broker, house and feed the five of them, and a bit of coin of a fortnight, seven years' labor was a fair price. Unless Hulse felt he should be more than a common laborer, which Denholm suspected he'd one day become, but wasn't warranted just now.

"Thank you for your offer, Mister Carew," Hulse said, jaw set. "I'll surely consider it."

Denholm frowned. He had the sense he'd insulted the man, but couldn't see how. He thought to offer Hulse his hand, but felt it wouldn't be accepted, so he simply nodded and turned to go. He left the rope stall and consulted his tablet. There was no one else on his list to interview as a laborer. Which left only the other list, the one that broke his heart to think on.

"Mister Carew, sir!"

Denholm turned. Hulse was calling him back, his wife standing next to him with the infant still in her arms.

"My wife tells me I may have misunderstood you." He gave a little smile. "Wouldn't be the first time she's seen things clearer than I."

A pain ran through Denholm, but he forced a smile. It wasn't Hulse's fault that Lynelle was gone and would never again tell him that he was missing someone's point. He forced the feeling down and walked back.

"The man before you made an offer of three years."

Denholm pursed his lips. "Don't see how he could. Three doesn't cover half of what your broker's asking."

"Three for him in the fields," Hulse's wife said, "three for me in the house, and three for each of the little ones when they're of an age to work."

Denholm wasn't shocked. It was a harsh offer but not unheard of to split an indenture over all the members of a family. Harshest for the children, though, for if Hulse signed the contract on their behalf now, they'd owe the three years and something for their room and board while they'd grown. And if that were the sort of offer Hulse was used to, then no wonder he'd been offended at Denholm's seven — thinking Denholm meant seven years indenture for every family member.

"I'd think you'd want to be home with your little ones, Mistress Hulse," he said, "and their time better spent in schooling. Be a shame if Seth Diebach's work on our learning core went to waste. Seven of *your* years, Mister Hulse, and I've no hold on the rest of your family." He offered his hand to Hulse. "It's no hard feelings on my side either way if you've no interest in the offer, sir, but I'm glad there'll be no misunderstanding."

Hulse took the offered hand. "A cottage, you say?"

Denholm smiled. "With a bit of land for a kitchen garden," he said to Hulse's wife.

Hulse and his wife shared a look. "Seven?"

"Aye."

"Done, then, and thank you, Mister Carew."

"Come along then and we'll tell the broker." Denholm hoisted two of their bags from the pile. "I've a wagon waiting near the chandlery gates."

After the indenture broker was notified and the contract recorded, Denholm walked them to his wagon and they loaded their bags.

"We'll be here in town until the Conclave is finished and then to my holding — I've tents near the amphitheater for us until then. It's not the most luxurious, I'm afraid."

"After a ship's hold, I'm sure it will be quite nice, Mister Carew, thank you."

"I've some ... one last thing to do here." He pulled some coins from his pocket. Hulse moved to wave it away, but Denholm held it out. "Two shillings the fortnight. Your first pay and a bit for a meal here in town while you wait for me to return — room and board, Mister Hulse, it's in the contract, yes?"

Hulse nodded and took the coins, raising a knuckle to his forehead. "Thank you, sir."

"There are food stalls down the street there beside the chandlery, but there's a decent pub or two beyond. The Lion has a fine roast most days, if they've not kept it on the spit too long. Come back here to the wagon after. My last bit of business shouldn't ... it'll not take but a short time."

Hulse nodded, but his wife frowned.

"I beg your pardon, Mister Carew, but is anything the matter?"

"Mercia —"

"It's all right, Mister Hulse, there's no harm in the asking." Denholm looked down and sighed. "My wife passed some months ago, Mistress Hulse."

She laid a hand on his arm. "I'm sorry."

"Thank you. We've a son, Lynelle and I." Denholm smiled. "He's a fine boy, but I can't watch him and work the holding both. There're women to help, but they have little ones of their own." Denholm paused. It was one thing to admit it was necessary, another to say the words, but there were things needed doing around the house that the women of the village hadn't the time for. There was always work enough to fill everyone's days. The thought of another woman in Lynelle's house, though, even just to cook and clean and care for Harlyn ... even that felt like a betrayal. "I've thought to find someone to help in the house and with the boy."

"There was a girl aboard ship, Mister Carew, that you may wish to speak to."

"Mercia," Hulse said, "it's not our place."

"No," Denholm said. "If you know her well, I'd admire your recommendation."

"Not well, no, but she seems a good person in need of a place."

"What world did she emigrate from?"

She paused. "The story's hers to tell, I think, Mister Carew, but you'd do well to speak with her. Don't judge her by the broker's records." She laid a hand on his arm and nodded to him. "Speak to the girl."

Denholm left the Hulses and went in search of the woman they'd spoken of. He reviewed her file on the way and was unimpressed despite the couple's words. This Levett woman had been transported, which was strike against her to begin with, but the charges were such that he didn't see how the Hulses could think he'd invite her onto the farm let alone into his very home.

Theft, assault — and against her employer, no less.

Moreover, she'd been aboard the indenture ships for almost a full year — near a dozen different colony worlds as the ship made its circuit around the Fringe, moving criminals and hopefuls from world to world. But to be so long aboard those ships? The cost of her indenture grew with every week aboard and to have received no offers?

Some holders on the Fringe would take murderers who'd barely escaped the gallows to work their lands.

Just how poorly did this girl interview?

TWENTY-THREE

"No."

Denholm froze. He was barely a step into the roped off square where the woman, girl, really, the record said she was but seventeen, sat on a canvas bag. She was reading from a small, well-worn tablet and hadn't even bothered to look up as he approached.

"I —"

"No," she said again, this time looking up at him. "I'll not take an offer from you." She waved a hand dismissively. "Move along with yourself."

Denholm blinked, still frozen in place. Of all the reactions to his approach, of all the introductions he could have imagined, being told to move along before he'd spoken a word hadn't even entered his mind as a possibility.

"Miss Levett, I think —"

The girl held up a hand to stop him. She set her tablet on her bag, stood, and smoothed her skirts.

"I've been a year aboard ship, sir — from fair, to fair, to fair — and there's much I've learned. First of it is that there are things, positions, worse than life aboard ship —" She gestured up at the sky "— with occasional fair days to read in the sun."

Denholm frowned. What on Earth was the girl talking about? He'd made no offer at all, no overtures, certainly not anything untoward.

"Miss Levett, I'm afraid you misunderstand —"

"I learned my lessons in the servants' quarters before all this — how hard it was when I had even a little power and options. Now? No, sir, my only power is whether to take a contract and I'll not be gulled again." She began ticking things off on her fingers. "No families with young men, none where the man leers while his wife stands by and ignores it —" She looked Denholm over. "— and certainly no bachelors."

Denholm almost laughed.

"No bachelors, sir. Your shirt's stained, your trousers are torn and go unmended, your beard's untrimmed, and I'll wager were you to slide off those boots I'll not see a matched pair of stockings. It's clear to me there's no woman in your house to take care of you and I'll be no man's doxy ... nor thought to be rescued for courtship. So ..." She frowned. "Sir, are you unwell?"

Denholm had found her reaction amusing at first, that she'd think he sought to buy her indenture for such nefarious purposes, but the litany had undone him. Had he really let himself go so much without Lynelle to care for him? And what would she think of it? Then those thoughts drove home to him that she was gone. That she'd never chide him for what he wore and send him off to change, never again.

He'd cried more than once since she'd passed, but always in private. Never where the hands or villagers could see, certainly not amongst his peers, not even at the funeral — it simply wasn't done. But there were tears on his cheeks now and he could feel the stares of those passing. They'd lose respect for him, a gentleman didn't show such emotions in public, but he didn't care — or if he did care, he couldn't make himself move to change it. He simply stood and cried until a single sob escaped him.

"Oh, sweet lord, what've I said?" The girl took his arm, looking around frantically. "Come here, sir, come here." She pulled him to her bag. "People're staring and I know your sort, you'll not want them to see this. Sit." She fairly shoved him down to sit on her bag and forced his tablet into his hands, then knelt a little distance away. "I'm sorry, sir, for whatever it is I said. Look down at your tablet and no one'll see. We're discussing terms and you're calculating the indenture, see? They'll never know different."

Denholm struggled to control himself.

"I am sorry, sir, I never meant for ..." She looked away and shook her head. "Oh, Julia Levett, if your wits were half as sharp as your tongue you'd have an easier life, no doubt."

Slowly Denholm gained control of himself. He cleared his throat and wiped his eyes, finally able to look up and glad to see that there was no large crowd of fellow holders staring at him as he'd feared.

"My apologies, Miss Levett, I don't know what came over me."

"No, sir, it's I who should ..." She half-smiled. "There's a powerful lot of sorries here and no end to them if we keep on, I think."

"Aye." Denholm wiped his eyes again and looked around, happy to see no one even staring. "And thank you. I've to spend the next few days in Conclave with these men, and I'd not have them see me so."

"It's a bit of silliness, it is, but I understand the way of it." She reached out tentatively, as though unsure, then grasped his arm. "I suspect now the particular mess that might be on the boot I've just tasted, but would you tell me?"

Much to his surprise, Denholm found himself talking. Not just the bare facts, but of how difficult life had been since Lynelle's death and his fears as well — things he'd told no one, not even Sewall Mylin, his closest friend on Dalthus. His fear for Harlyn growing up with a different woman from the village in the house to clean and watch him each day, his fear that anyone he brought into the house to care for the lad would be seen to take the place of Lynelle, that his fear of *that* would mean the boy grew up cared for by those who didn't truly love him. He knew how to be a father to the lad, to teach him the land and what to be a man. He'd never thought Lynelle wouldn't be there for the other things. More to his surprise than the words was that there were no more tears.

When he'd finished, Levett rose to her feet and held out a hand. He took it and stood. She picked up her bag, then frowned and looked him over.

"All right, then, let's be about it." She held her bag out for him to carry. "And I'd be pleased did you call me Julia, sir, if I'm to keep house for you."

"THERE WAS NO THEFT," Julia said as they left the indenture agent, having made their agreement in a whirl that caused Denholm to wonder what it was he'd just agreed to, and made their way through the crowds to where Denholm had left the Hulses, "but, aye, there was assault — if defending myself must be called that. It was the son what tried to take what wasn't his to take and me defending from it. Course that was turned all around when we're before the magistrate and it's me accused of stealing some trifle and attacking him when he found me at it. So it was prison or transport for me and I was fed full of the Harnsey system for good and all."

For some reason Denholm believed her. She had a stiff, no nonsense feel about her that didn't lend itself to thoughts she'd do something like steal from anyone, much less an employer. That and her trying to send him on his way at first, saying she'd not take a place with a bachelor, oddly made him trust her word. He started to speak to tell her there'd be none of that sort of thing happening in his household, but she waved it away.

"I'll not steal from you and you'll not take liberties. So long as we stick to that there'll be no assaulting, neither. So may we leave the matter lie?"

Denholm nodded. He began to get the impression that the incident she described had gone a bit further than liberties before she'd managed to beat off her attacker, but also that she had no wish to speak of it.

TWENTY-FOUR

The open-air amphitheater on the outskirts of Landing was almost full when Denholm arrived. He made his way through the crowd to where he'd arranged to meet Sewall Mylin.

"I didn't think you'd make it," Mylin said by way of greeting.

"Almost didn't bother," Denholm said. "We could handle all these decisions with votes from our homes, why gather everyone together?"

Mylin looked at him oddly. "There's some like to see their peers in person once in a year. Or their neighbors, come to that."

"I —" Denholm sighed. "You're right, Sewall, I'm sorry. I've been a poor neighbor these last months ... and a poorer friend."

Mylin grasped his shoulder. "You're grieving. Elora and I understand, but we do wish you'd let us help you more."

Denholm nodded. He understood Mylin's desire to help, he'd feel the same if the situations were reversed, but he did wish people wouldn't seem to dwell on it so.

He gestured with his tablet to change the subject.

"Still, could we not have voted on some of these from our homes? First is a motion to rename Landing for Bailie Arthur — while I'm glad to have our port no longer named the same as so many other worlds', and certainly to see his sacrifice honored, is it something we all need to gather together to decide?"

"There's a bit more than that on the agenda, have you not read it?"

"Not all, no."

"Well, Harting's made a proposal that's not minor — and that my Elora's like to skin him for."

"Harting? That dog of Coalson's?"

Mylin nodded.

"What's he on about then?" Denholm searched the Conclave agenda and soon found it. He read and frowned. "Is the man mad?"

"You'll not support it then?"

"Of course not. It's ridiculous."

"Some don't see it so. There was enough support to bring it to a vote — it was a close-run thing, but it's on the agenda now." He looked away. "Another respected voice in opposition might have made the difference there."

Denholm felt the sting of the rebuke, but Mylin had a point. This change might affect his family and Denholm hadn't even been aware of it. If he'd paid even a bit of attention to the notices the last several months, then he might have spoken out about it. He'd not even bothered to vote on whether it should be brought before the conclave — something that took only a simple majority of those voting, not the two-thirds the change to the Charter would require to pass.

"Loftus is speaker this year?" Denholm asked as a man walked onto the stage and took his place at the podium.

"His name came up," Mylin said with a shrug. "Not many want the job."

They quieted as Loftus at the podium called for attention and brought the Conclave to order. The first bits of business passed with little or no discussion — renaming Landing to Port Arthur, a special assessment of the Holders to order a new communication and positioning satellite constellation to replace those destroyed by the pirates, and a series of notices, more courtesies than anything else, from holders planning to open up new lands for development.

"Item number sixteen on the agenda," Loftus called out, "prompted by the Charter, a motion for the Conclave to change from annual to every five years. This measure requires a two-thirds majority to pass. Speakers for or against?"

Loftus' call was met with silence. The colonists understood the need people had to fill up their time and appear useful. They'd seen enough of full-time legislatures who felt they had to justify their existence through ever more detailed laws and regulations, and had no desire to repeat the pattern on their new home. Even though they were both the legislature and the electorate, as only the original shareholders had a say in the running of the colony, they knew some of them might be tempted to fill their time with making laws if they met annually forever. They'd written into the colony's charter that one of the items on each annual conclave's agenda would be a motion for them to say enough is enough and space their sessions out more.

"With no calls to speak," Loftus said, "we will proceed to the vote. Please vote in the affirmative to change this Conclave's meetings to a five-year schedule, in the negative for it to remain annual."

Denholm frowned and eyed the buttons on his tablet, before making his decision. His lands weren't so far from Landing, now Port Arthur, that it was a hardship to come each year, still surely with all of human history to pull from they'd had enough laws from the start?

He glanced at Mylin and raised an eyebrow.

Mylin raised his tablet so Denholm could see and mashed his thumb onto the "Aye" button forcefully.

"There's many in this lot who should tend to their own business and leave others' alone," he said, "this next bit's a sign of that."

Denholm nodded. "We could have erased half the Charter at the start and simply said, 'Neither hurt anyone nor steal his things.'"

Mylin laughed. "Devil's in the details, though."

"I suppose."

"With forty-one percent Ayes, fifty-nine percent Nays," Loftus announced shortly, "the motion fails to carry."

Mylin shrugged. "Perhaps next year."

"Item number seventeen on the agenda," Loftus called. "A proposal by Nelson Harting, seconded by Rashae Coalson. Amendments as to the Charter's Articles of Inheritance. Speaking in favor will be Holder Harting, opposed Holder Bocook. Each will have fifteen minutes to speak."

"Bocook?" Denholm whispered to Mylin. "Whose choice was that?"

"She's been the most vocal against it."

They watched as the two Holders gained the stage and stood behind Loftus.

"Is that best, do you think?"

Mylin shrugged. "It's done now."

On the stage Harting had moved to the podium.

"I'm supposed to summarize the change," he said. "Don't know why that's needed, when you can just read it, but ... I'm proposing that we change the Charter to protect our lands and keep the inheritance straight. It's not but a small change, but I think we've all seen how important it is. Way it reads is all the references there in the Charter's Articles of Inheritance, where it says 'eldest child' gets changed to 'eldest son', see? Then there's added this bit about if there are no sons, that things go to the oldest girl's husband." There were murmurs growing in the crowd, but Harting went on as though oblivious to them. "And if there's none of him at the time of inheritance, then the shares and property go back to the colony and the rest of us can bid on them at the next Conclave." He looked up. "See?"

"Nelson Harting!" the woman on the stage shouted loud enough to be heard by all, as Harting had the podium's microphone. "I've spent this last week behind a plow and you're still the biggest horse's ass I can remember seeing in all my days!"

"Now, Lillee," Loftus said, "you'll have your chance to speak in opposition, just let Nelson finish, will you? We went over this!"

The woman clenched her jaw and crossed her arms.

"Silliness to be talking about it at all," she said, but took a step back.

Harting looked up, scanned the crowd, then back at his tablet. He seemed to not know what to say next, but a muted *ping* could be heard over the speakers. Harting frowned at his tablet, then leaned toward the microphone.

"I've a wish to yield the rest of my time to Holder Coalson, if I may," he said, looking up hopefully.

Rashae Coalson was already stepping onto the stage as Loftus nodded assent. Harting bolted for the stage's edge as though grateful to be out of the crowd's view.

Coalson straightened his shoulders and looked out over the crowd.

"We all know how important inheritance is to the colony's future," Coalson went on. "We knew it when we drew up the Charter to keep all our lands together. The holders' shares and land go to one heir, they can't be split up. That protects us from the dilution we've seen in other colonies, where three thousand voting holders become ten thousand in a generation, and then more. Look around you. You know the men here — know which of them you can trust. Do you want to come here one day and find thousands of strangers?"

Denholm looked around at the crowd. Most were shaking their heads now, but this was a settled issue, not part of the proposed amendment. The Charter already limited voting to shareholders and provided that the holdings could not be split amongst heirs. Coalson was simply going over what they'd already agreed to, getting the audience behind him and in the habit of agreeing. It was a tactic Denholm knew well, but there was little he could do to counter it from the crowd and he suspected Lillee Bocook wouldn't have the patience for it.

"And those colonies who've opened up the franchise to all? Do you want to see that here?" Coalson went on. There were more murmurs from the crowd, but this time of agreement. "An hundred thousand former indentures? Transported thieves, murderers, rapists, their indentured time done and free to vote? To make decisions for you and your families — do you wish to see that come to Dalthus?"

Now people were muttering and some actually shouting "No!" in response to Coalson's words.

Mylin turned to Denholm. "What does that have to do with —"

"Nothing." Denholm shook his head as he listened. "Not a thing. But they'll be fearful already when he speaks about these changes."

"Well we all voted on the Charter before we came here and agreed," Coalson said. "We set it up to avoid those things. This is our world, bought and paid for with everything we'd earned in our lives. The indentures know what our laws are here — if they find it's not to their liking, they're free to leave and try their hand at another world. No one's forced to stay on Dalthus, are they?"

"And here it'll come," Denholm whispered. Coalson had the crowd with him now, they were listening to every word and responding as one, much as Coalson must have intended.

"We didn't know everything when we wrote the Charter, though. We didn't know how hard this world would be, nor how much work there'd be for us on the lands or in our households, nor what changes those things would cause.

"So what happens now, if my eldest son wishes to marry Harting's eldest daughter, eh? With them both inheriting the lands?" Coalson waved a hand at Harting in the front row of the crowd. "And then their son inherits? Well, then he's the vote of both our families' shares, doesn't he? Do you want to see that either? Families joining and taking on more and more power over you?"

More mutters of "no" came from the crowd.

"When we lived in the Core we were all successful. We could afford all the technology of the Core. It took minutes to get anywhere in the city, hours to anywhere on the planet. We had machines to do the cleaning and the shops to purchase anything we might need."

"Those are luxuries we've given up here, though. We all know the changes we've had to make. The segregation of work. The men're in the fields and the women in the homes." He held up a hand to fore-stall Bocook who'd begun to step forward. "I know, Lillee, you've worked your lands as hard as anyone since your Nelson passed, but if he was living it'd be him in the fields, do you deny it?"

Bocook's nostrils flared, but she didn't speak.

Still Coalson was speaking no more than the truth. It was a traditional division of labor that had happened on virtually every colony world, especially in the early generations. There'd even been a lecture on it put on by the survey company that had sold Dalthus to the colonists, though only a few had attended. They'd called it Colonial Regression Syndrome, and given all the reasons for it.

"It's no more than the truth," Coalson went on, echoing Denholm's thoughts, "and it only makes sense, doesn't it? Until we've all those conveniences from back in the Core, while being sure of dinner means keeping a kitchen garden and plucking our own chickens, it's simply how we live. And those are the skills our daughters learn, because those are the skills they'll use."

There was some murmuring at this, but not much, mostly from the few women who, like Lillee Bocook, had found themselves suddenly without the partners who'd come with them to Dalthus.

Coalson went on, but Denholm couldn't bring himself to listen any longer.

"What's your sense of this, will it pass?" he asked Mylin.

"It'll be close, but it will." Mylin nodded. "Catherine Arthur's had a hard time of it since Bailie and their sons were killed. And there's what happened at the Welding holding still fresh in their minds. They see that little Amette in their daughters and it scares them."

Denholm sighed. Mention of the Weldings brought his own loss of Lynelle to mind.

Freda Welding had passed much as Lynelle had, in sudden complications giving birth. Her husband, Elston, had seen her body washed and laid out for burial, then made his way to the barn and eased his pain with the taste of a flechette gun. Denholm could almost understand his act, but Elston Welding had left behind others who depended on him. Aside from his indentures, there were his five children.

Amette had been the eldest, but a bare fourteen years old, and ill-suited for running the lands. She'd tried, though, thinking it was her duty and refusing help from neighbors, telling them that all was fine on the holding. It had helped her deception that the Weldings had settled so far from their nearest neighbor and that all the holder families were so busy with their own lands.

The harvest went poorly but still the Welding children asked for no assistance until, at mid-Winter, the holding stopped responding at all.

Neighbors came finally and found nothing but a looted farmstead and the bodies of the Welding children.

The indentures, starving, in all likelihood and afraid they'd be blamed, had taken all that was left and run off into the wilderness of Dalthus.

"Could just have easily been an eldest boy there," Denholm said.

"It doesn't matter," Mylin said. "They think this will stop it happening again, and all the other ills Coalson's warning of. They don't want to know about what's right or fair, they want a solution to keep that from happening again." He shrugged. "No matter that such a law wouldn't have stopped it — folks want to feel like it would have, regardless."

"What's Rashae's point in this? He must see some benefit to himself."

Mylin shrugged. "Perhaps he's just being a bitter bastard — it's what he's good at."

Denholm looked around at the crowd. He could tell by their faces and their response to Coalson, still speaking, how the vote would go.

"No, there must be more to it than just that."

Mylin shrugged again. "They're young, but the man does have more sons than he knows what to do with, come to that."

Denholm frowned.

"Pass the law, then try to marry off his sons to those as have only daughters?" Mylin continued.

"That's a long game to play, and not at all certain."

"There's more than one girl on planet who'd rather farm alone than marry a Coalson, perhaps he means to force the issue."

Denholm laughed.

"No, he's likely not behind it, I agree, but it's not beyond him to think to use it so."

On the platform, Coalson had yielded to Bocook, who was haranguing the crowd over the stupidity of the proposal. Denholm felt her frustration, but knew it was the wrong tactic. If people liked an idea, telling them they were stupid for it rarely changed their mind.

"You could ask to speak," Mylin said. "There are many who'd listen to you."

"I don't know, Sewall." He looked around at the crowd. "Would they?"

"You're respected." Mylin paused. "Lynelle was respected. She'd have some things to say about this, I think."

Denholm's throat tightened, but his lips twitched. "My Lynelle would be on stage chiding Lillee Bocook for her excess of moderation."

"I do think you could sway them," Mylin insisted.

"Perhaps ..." Denholm considered it. It was a silly, pointless change to make. He didn't want to get more involved in the politics of the colony — didn't want there to *be* politics of the colony, truth be told — but perhaps he should.

He pulled out his tablet, preparing to query Bocook to allow him a bit of her time to speak — a few words surely wouldn't go amiss — then stopped and frowned as he saw someone moving toward him.

Rashae Coalson had left the platform and was working his way through the crowd, stopping here and there to shake hands and speak a word. Denholm was surprised to see the man headed in his direction and more so when Coalson caught his eye.

TWENTY-FIVE

"Carew."

Denholm eyed Coalson warily. He was aware of Mylin taking a step away and to the side, hand on his belt near his knife. He doubted Coalson's plan was to attack him here in the Conclave, but appreciated the support. He also noted that, despite Bocook's ongoing speech from the platform, those in the crowd around him were paying more attention to him and Coalson.

"Coalson."

"We've had our differences, but I wanted to offer my sentiments on the loss of your wife. There are few men I'd wish such a thing on," Coalson said, his eyes intent. "Your son is well?"

Mylin's eyes narrowed and Denholm found the man's phrasing odd, but given their differences and past he understood it might be hard for Coalson to offer condolences. His throat tightened, but he managed to keep his voice level.

"Harlyn's well — and your own sons?"

"My eldest is a bit womanish, but the next, Daviel, is shaping up nicely." Coalson shrugged. "The others are too young to tell." He nodded toward the platform. "You have some thoughts on this proposal, I suppose?"

"I do," Denholm said. "Though they're likely not yours."

Coalson grunted. "I thought you'd see the sense of supporting this — it only codifies what we all know to be true, after all."

Denholm raised an eyebrow.

"The girls aren't suited to the task of running a holding," Coalson went on. He nodded toward the platform. "Oh, not those like Bocook — she does an adequate job, I suppose — but she's an aberration. No, most are like that Welding girl — ill-suited to the hardships of running more than a household. It takes a firm hand to control the indentures, don't you see that?"

"I've found a bit of kindness and mutual respect works well enough with the hands," Denholm said.

"With yours, I suppose," Coalson said, "but you've expanded more slowly, and picked and chose your hands. Some of us have harder men on our lands who understand other ways. There's —"

"We were warned about this nonsense before we came," Mylin interrupted. "There's a name for it, even."

Coalson waved a hand dismissively. "Yes, that 'Colonial Regression Syndrome' nonsense — and did you never wonder if there's not a reason for it, rather than just naming it so? As if it's some disease we all catch from being out here on the Fringe? Easy for them to look down on us in the Core, where they've manufactures and hospitals aplenty, when we colonies revert to older ways, but why do we, then? Why is it so prevalent they have a name for the thing? Perhaps, just ask yourself, is it not because those old ways work best out here?"

He turned to face Mylin, then back to Denholm. "Tell me, is it not so on your holding? And wasn't it on yours, Carew, before your wife passed? Didn't the work fall out naturally between you? Doesn't it still with the indentures who have families? The men go out into the fields and forests and mines, while the women tend to the home." He shook his head. "There's no shame in it. I'm certainly not saying one's of more worth than the other — lord knows I'd rather someone else pluck the chickens, to be sure — but when it happens so naturally, can you say it's wrong?"

Denholm wondered at Coalson's apparent need to convince him. The man had strung more words together without damning Denholm's eyes to hell than he'd ever experienced before.

"Natural or not, it was our choice," Denholm said, "and the choice of those on my lands who do so. I'd not see someone forced into what they don't want or aren't suited for, but neither will I see them denied it if they are."

That, he realized, was what was really wrong with the Charter as it stood. Not that the planet's inheritance law needed to be restricted to the eldest son, but that 'eldest' business was a mistake as well.

"The trouble with the Welding girl wasn't that she was unsuited to running the lands as a girl, but that she was unsuited to running the lands. I remember the Welding children, and there was a younger daughter who had a good head on her shoulders. Given time and a bit of guidance she'd have grown into it."

Denholm could see Mylin pondering that as well.

"Look you, Coalson," he said, "I do agree with keeping the lands and shares together, but shouldn't a man be able to choose which of his children will take it on after him? You just seemed to say yourself that your second son, Daviel, might be more suited to the task."

In truth, Coalson had called his first son "womanish", a characterization Denholm found distasteful, but Coalson seemed to think it important.

And this is why I don't like politics. It's too bloody easy to fall into preying on others' prejudices in an effort to convince them.

He pulled out his tablet, prepared to request Bocook allow him to say a few words and propose exactly that change instead of what Coalson supported.

Coalson's face grew hard.

"I'd hoped we could find common ground in this, at least, after what happened to your wife."

Denholm froze. What could Coalson possibly mean by that now?

What did this ridiculous change in the Charter have to do with Lynelle's death?

"Isn't this exactly what killed her, Carew? Out in a storm, working with the stock instead safe inside?"

Mylin stepped forward. "Now, see here —"

"Do you wonder about it?" All Coalson's previous tone of friendliness and reason had vanished, replaced by the bitter hatred Denholm had come to associate with him. "If you'd kept her safely in her place, would she still be alive now?"

Denholm's vision blurred, his throat tightened, and he spun around to blindly force his way through the crowd and out of the tent — it was either that or wrap his hands around Coalson's throat and assuage his anger and sorrow that way.

The truth was that Coalson's words struck far too close to home and the pain of Lynelle's death was far too recent for him to have any perspective about it.

He had wondered that very thing. Not in so many words, certainly not in so hateful a tone, but he had wondered.

What if he'd kept one or two of the hands back that night, despite Lynelle's insistence they were needed in the village? Surely the village would have made do without? What if he'd insisted she remain safe and warm inside the farmhouse?

Despite Doctor Purdue's assurances that neither the work nor being outside in the storm had made a significant difference, Denholm still blamed himself. For bringing her here, away from the safety and security of the Core. For not keeping her safe, as he thought he should. For everything.

"Denholm —"

Mylin caught up with him outside the Conclave tent, grasping his arm to stop his flight.

"No, Sewall, I'm done." He pulled out his tablet and ran fingers across it. "That man, those ... it's everything I hate and I'm through with it." He swiped a finger on his tablet to send Mylin his proxy for the voting. "There, you've my proxy to vote my shares on the rest of the issues — vote as you see fit."

He shrugged off Mylin's hand and started toward where the Hulses, Julia Levett, and the other new indentures waited for the long trek back to his holding.

They'd worked so hard to get here and build something, he and Lynelle, and it had all turned so wrong. He'd lost so much and felt he didn't have the energy to give to the colony at large anymore. It was enough to care for his lands, the indentures who looked to him, and Harlyn.

"Will you leave the running of the colony to the likes of Coalson, then, Denholm?"

"I'm done with it, Sewall. I've my own lands to run and a son to raise."

A NOTE FROM THE AUTHOR

Thank you for reading *Planetfall*.

I hope you enjoyed it.

If you did and would like to further support the series, please consider leaving a review on the purchase site or a review/rating on Goodreads — if you received *Planetfall* as a free gift for signing up for the mailing list, you can still leave a review :). Reviews are the lifeblood of independent authors and let other readers know what books they might enjoy.

If you'd like to be notified of future releases, please consider following me on Twitter or Facebook, or joining my mailing list. The mailing list is limited to no more than one or two updates a month on the status of forthcoming books and the occasional update on what I'm reading myself.

Planetfall was written for those fans of the Alexis Carew series who wanted to explore the lives of some of the other characters on Alexis' home world during the time before she was born, as well as some more world-building around the colonization and indenture processes of the Fringe Worlds, something that's hard to do from Alexis' perspective in the Navy.

I started writing *Planetfall* in the fall of 2014, even before *Into the Dark* was published. *Mutineer* was complete and ready to go to the editors, *The Little Ships* was but a glimmer in some nether-recess of my brain, and I wanted to write something that would explore all those things I just mentioned.

Since then, though, the outline for "*Planetfall*", which was originally planned as a single, 20,000-word novella, grew to over 60,000 words — and I made the decision to publish it in two parts:

Part One, this volume, covering the first few years of the colonization and up until the time Alexis' father, Harlyn, is born.

Part Two, forthcoming later this year or in 2017, showing a slightly more mature colony and introducing the second generation.

Splitting it up will allow me to release the parts as I finish them, and, really, they are two separate stories — this, from Denholm's perspective, and the second from Harlyn's.

It's also, I have to admit, one of the more depressing stories in the series to write … given Alexis' family's history, I suppose there's no way it could have been any different. Still, for as brief a time as I had with some of these characters, they came to mean a great deal to me.

I actually wrote the scene where Lynelle dies while I was on a cruise … so picture me there on the Promenade deck, laptop on the table before me, fruity-rum drink close to hand … with tears streaming down my face …

"Sir? Sir, are you all right?"
 "I just killed someone I love. Leave me alone."
 "…"

Take care in the questions you ask writers.

J.A. Sutherland
 Washington, DC
 February 19, 2016

ALSO BY J.A. SUTHERLAND

To be notified when new releases are available, follow J.A. Sutherland on Facebook (https://www.facebook.com/jasutherlandbooks/), Twitter (https://twitter.com/JASutherlandBks), or subscribe to the author's newsletter (http://www.alexiscarew.com/list).

Alexis Carew

Into the Dark

Mutineer

The Little Ships

HMS Nightingale

Privateer

The Queen's Pardon

Planetfall (prequel)

Spacer, Smuggler, Pirate, Spy

Spacer

Smuggler (coming 2019)

Trade Runs

Running Start (coming 2019)

Running Scared (coming 2019)

Running on Empty (coming 2019)

Short Stories

Mad Cow

Dark Artifice

(Writing as Richard Grantham)

Of Dubious Intent

ABOUT THE AUTHOR

J.A. Sutherland spends his time sailing the Bahamas on a 43' 1925 John G. Alden sailboat called Little Bit ...

Yeah ... no. In his dreams.

Reality is a townhouse in Orlando with a 90 pound huskie-wolf mix who won't let him take naps.

When not reading or writing, he spends his time on roadtrips around the Southeast US searching for good barbeque.

Mailing List: http://www.alexiscarew.com/list

To contact the author:
www.alexiscarew.com
sutherland@alexiscarew.com

Made in the USA
Middletown, DE
09 December 2020